Operation Dancing Dog

Operation Dancing Dog

by James M. Fox

Walker and Company
New York

First published in the United States of America in 1974 by the Walker Publishing Company, Inc.

Published simultaneously in Canada by Fitzhenry & Whiteside, Limited, Toronto.

ISBN: 0-8027-5292-6

Library of Congress Catalog Card Number: 73-90391

Printed in the United States of America.

10 9 8 7 6 5 4 3 2 1

DISINFORMATION

TANGIER, FRIDAY NIGHT, JULY 16.

Marcia Ellis collects people. She can well afford such an expensive hobby, for she has the kind of money that is managed by investment bankers and by corporation lawyers on three continents. She is a statuesque and very nicely preserved widow lady in her sixties who has always lived to please herself, and who comes on like an extremely pleasant hostess once she has collected you.

Some of the specimens she acquires are questionable as to rarity or value. This is not surprising, since her tastes are catholic, her appetites a trifle strong. She likes to collect every day, and certainly not less than several times a week. Sitting beside her, watching her make a selection was no novelty to me; she had acquired me all the way back in September '52. She'd even listen to occasional suggestions from me. ". . .These kids are pretty young."

"You really think so, Steve?"

"Well, not if you mean innocent, no. But in every other sense. And it would help if they had any sort of talent."

There were four of them, calling themselves the Strawberry Preserves Conspiracy. This was supposed to signify something enormously portentous but had turned out to be just another college group making the tourist scene in an old Volkswagen,

3

presenting counterculture songs. On Marcia Ellis's mosaic-tiled patio under an apricot Moroccan moon, these sounded singularly unconvincing. Audience reaction from the thirty-odd of us in dinner dress restrained itself to chilly courtesy.

"I rather like the girl," said Marcia, and pursed her lips judicially.

The girl struck me as without merit. She was overweight and underage. She needed a shampoo and, probably, a long, hot shower.

"At least she won't be shy," I said. But Marcia had already turned away to whisper in Sven Wahlstrom's ear. He was a recent acquisition, possibly as recent as a day or two—one of her better specimens, a Danish count, still in his thirties, crew-cut, whipcord-slim, Polaroid-monocled. I knew something about him I was fairly sure she didn't, but it made no difference: Marcia wasn't political, as far as I could tell in twenty years. She had no time. Not with her villas in Juan-les-Pins, Bermuda, Acapulco, and Kauai, and with a two thousand-ton, thirty-five-knot Diesel yacht to bounce among them. And, of course, with her collection to keep up.

The Tangier villa sits behind a ten-foot fieldstone wall in something like ten acres on The Mountain, right next door to what had been the Sultan Mulay Hafid's residence before the French had leaned on him in 1912. It has a view that may not be quite as sensational as any in the world, but it competes for honors in that league. It also has a Roman fountain, A.D. 156, with landscaping to match; but, as you might expect, the furnishings and indoor plumbing are one hundred percent Yankee import from Chicago, Illinois. Marcia Ellis favors comfort and convenience over style.

The Strawberry Preserves Conspiracy was into "When Johnny Comes Marching Home," with special lyrics that would never get past the Supreme Court, and with not particularly special vocal talent or guitar work. That seemed to conclude the program. It received a spatter of polite applause and a small, girlish raspberry, behind my back. I glanced around at the producer with a grin of sympathy. She had a table by herself: Miss Yuri Franklin, twenty-eight, third generation Japanese-American. Born in a relocation camp in World War II, the child of an assistant warden and an inmate. Stanford '63, majored in anthropology. Profession: call girl, *poule de luxe*. All this according to my index file card, back at the hotel. The file itself contained at least a dozen photos, some of them in color, none that did much justice to her almond blossom daintiness, or gave more than a hint of the intangibles, the tinkling silver laugh, the misty fragrance of her scent.

Marcia Ellis stared at us over one shoulder, half-indignantly. "What's wrong? I dig young people, don't you?"

Wahlstrom said: "Miss Franklin is unlikely to debate the point with you, my dear. And Mr. Harvester appears unwilling."

"Nothing to debate," I said. "Resolved: we dig young people. Babies who wear diapers, or college kids who should. It's not their fault if they're not given toilet training."

Wahlstrom focused his green monocle and sneered at me. Marcia said: "Steve, that's so unkind. Don't you believe in everybody's right of self-expression anymore?"

"Not everybody's, no. One has to qualify. I think you know that very well."

"Qualification by whose rules?" asked Yuri Franklin mockingly.

The question was unanswerable, but Leon de Bas supplied an answer. He loomed over us, all five feet six, two hundred fifty pounds of him; bald skull, bland moonface, treble chin, shrewd little chipmunk eyes. Born 1917 in Léopoldville, Belgian Congo, said the file card. Mining engineer, retired, net worth in excess of a hundred million Belgian francs. KGB agent. Homosexual. "A frivolous polemic," he advised us.

"Self-expression is a common need, although its exercise is normally offensive. To the many or the few. There are, of course, exceptions." Nonchalantly waving his cigar, he indicated the two ladies in our company.

Wahlstrom came after me about an hour later, in the lavatory. "May I see you privately for a few moments, Major Harvester?" The military title was an eyebrow raiser. I'd removed it with my air force uniform in January 1946.

"This isn't very private."

"I believe you know this house." He sounded dry without deliberate insinuation. "There's a guest room on the second floor that should be vacant." What he meant was that he'd just moved out of it.

I hadn't visited Marcia's workshop in a very long time, but she'd made no changes; drapery and rugs in golden beige, the king-size velvet divan a warm burgundy and piled with cushions. Four Picasso etchings in a step-up pattern on the wall facing the bed, two of them boy-girl, two girl-girl. Portable bar and ice box, concealed stereo and movie screen. The rheostatted lighting scheme had been designed to flatter female skin texture and tone. The balcony was suitable for sunbathing. Wahlstrom had turned on the cold water in the bath when I walked in, three minutes after him; I doubted that there was a hearing aid around, but he was right to play it safe, of course. He leaned against the shower cabin and allowed his monocle to dangle while he made a study of his manicure. "I'm only trying to make sure that we don't get into each other's way," he said.

"If you mean Marcia, don't give it another thought."

"You know exactly what I mean, Major." He seemed to be annoyed with me.

I put one foot up on the rock crystal bidet and squeezed my chin for him. It didn't make me happy that he was aware of me at all. "I'm not on active service. You are. You're a captain in the Danish army and attached to NATO Brussels, Section Six, counterintelligence. Maybe you heard that I was in that line of work myself. But that was in War Two, my friend, while you were still in kneepants. So what makes you think . . ."

He cut me short. "Excuse me, Major, I just don't have time for this." His eyes came up to mine, and they were ice-blue with impatience. "Will you tell me what you're doing in Tangier?"

"Of course, why not? I'm what the critics commonly refer to as a minor novelist. I also write for magazines like *Holiday* and *Esquire*. Mrs. Ellis, as you know, is an old flame of mine, but I've been staying at the Rif Hotel. What's your excuse?"

"Since you insist on fencing with me . . ." He controlled himself and shrugged it off. "Are you concerned in any manner with Leon de Bas?" he asked me reasonably. "If you are, we might perhaps assist each other."

"No, I'm not."

It happened that I wasn't quite so sure—it might have been more accurate to say I hoped not. Wahlstrom, visibly displeased, leaned down over the tub to turn the water off. For no good reason I held up a hand to stop him; charity comes pretty hard to me, most of the time. "You're operating on your own?" He nodded. "I suppose you realize he's a bad customer."

"Here in Morocco there is nothing I can do about the man," he said, almost indifferently.

"But you never know," I said. "There's always a Dutch freighter or a French destroyer in the harbor. Sailors have a great deal of appeal to people like de Bas."

Wahlstrom said coolly: "Yes, they do." He reached down for the faucet, changed his mind, and tucked his monocle in place to stare at me. "What's Dancing Dog, please, Major Harvester?"

If he was looking for a guilty start or for a gleam of interest, he got no satisfaction. I am one-eighth Navajo and play a fair amount of poker, but there was no need for careful impassivity. "Sorry, I've no idea. Sounds like the code name for an operation. One of theirs."

"Leon de Bas made us an offer of exposure. In exchange for temporary immunity. He wants to visit Belgium and deal with family affairs."

"No good, of course," I said. "Disinformation. That's what he'd come up with, something that sounds fine but isn't, and that can't be checked out all the way. Or not for a long time."

"We'll probably accept," said Wahlstrom, casually. "I shall recommend it."

That I could believe, but not that anything would come of it. You hear about such deals, but they don't happen. A defector may be genuine or not. In either case he's squeezed out like a lemon, and the rind goes in the garbage can. I said: "You might as well turn off the water, captain," and walked out on him. Downstairs, the party hadn't picked up a great deal of horsepower for all the liquid fuel that was being pumped to it. Most of the guests had left the terrace for the air-conditioned comforts of the grand salon. The night was sultry, and oppressive with the redolence of goat dung, rotting fruit, and patchouli that is North Africa. I wandered out in it, into the garden, and sat down beside the Roman fountain on a marble bench. At fifty-four you're likely to have got into the habit of relaxing when you can and looking back over your shoulder when you should.

A little more than twenty years ago, three members of the Princeton Club were having lunch. Across the table they discovered they were tired of what was going on: Korea, and the so-called Cold War, and the massive Soviet espionage and propaganda *apparat*. They were a railroad president, a banker, and an advertising man, or so the story goes, and they had friends who also took exception to their country being shoved around. It was decided to put up a little money and shove back.

They called in Jimmy Dexter, who'd been an executive for Wild Bill Donovan in the old OSS, and who was then handling public relations for a few corporate clients in New York —the type of corporations that prefer *not* to be mentioned in the press. Dexter proposed a system of procedure, named it Project A—intentionally colorless—and was employed to carry on with it.

He hired a dozen social misfits with experience, such as me. We went to work, mostly in Western Europe and in Africa, assembling local teams of double-dealers and informers, figuring out blocking plays and counterjabs. We weren't supposed to touch the rough stuff with our own lily-white hands—just buy the facts, coordinate them, improvise a handle for them, buy it fitted on. There is a section of the CIA that operates this way, but it is badly handicapped. Its members are enmeshed in agency directives, curbed by civil service regulations, harassed by the State Department, the Department of Defense, the "watchdog" committees of Congress.

We just spent the project's money and stayed out of trouble. Paymasters are always popular. Nobody shoots at them or tries to put them into jail.

Of course the Russians and their local friends had never loved us very much. The stuff we purchased was embarrassing to them. We got a copy of the Mig-19 and one of the Mig-21, complete with pilots, in the year they first came out. We bought a flock of foreign ministers' assistants, minor Warsaw Pact officials, African commanding generals, and a colonel in the KGB. We paid for passage through the iron curtain of East German scientists, Siberian prisoners, and Russian literary manuscripts. We frustrated a handful of political assassinations and persuaded two of the assassins to defect. Some of the people we were dealing with proved to be poor insurance risks, but we ourselves needed to worry only about never talking to strange gentlemen who offered us a bag of sweets. In twenty years, you either pick up this technique or you come down with ulcers. Some of us were regularly dieting on milk and Gelusil.

From Washington they'd leaned on Jimmy Dexter with the FBI, the first six months or so, until they came to the astonishing conclusion that he wasn't talking to the newspapers. Then they decided Project A was no more dangerous politically, or illegal, than a group of multimillionaires insisting upon overpaying on their income tax.

In twenty years, this was my sixth or seventh visit to Tangier. I'd known the place when it was still a so-called international zone: run by the banks and half a dozen foreign consuls, overrun by crooks, packed with corruption like a boil. In '56, when it was taken over by the kingdom of Morocco, there were changes made: the consuls reassigned to checking cargo manifests, the street cleaners given a cut in wages with predictable results. Most of the tourist traffic, irritated by the new officiousness of customs and police, backed up in Spain. But there was still the climate, and the Kasbah, and there were the banks, the ever-loving, wheeler-dealer banks where you can get financed if you're a diamond smuggler or an able revolutionary with good prospects. Or if you should want to build your own atomic bomb. We'd sorted out a problem with those banks, on one or two occasions, but this time I had no business for them. My business in Tangier, this time, was to buy a king.

I'd met him earlier that evening. He was Marcia's guest of honor, though I doubted very much that she intended to collect him—he just wasn't a good specimen. He drank like a Russian, and he was a religious maniac, and Yuri Franklin had him, had latched on to him at least six months ago. I saw her point of view, or what seemed fairly sure to be her point of view. Any professional likes status. An interior decorator in Los Angeles would rather do a house for Cary Grant than twenty villas in a middle-class development. Actually, Carol Rudolf Ferdinand von Hohenzollern-Sigmaringen looked a lot like Cary Grant. He was about as tall, and only slightly heavier. His hair was gray and styled about the same, and he was similarly hawk-faced, with an air of typical, insouciant British-actor dissipation. He dressed beautifully and behaved with mannered arrogance. No doubt about it, he would be considered a desirable protector by a sensibly ambitious working girl.

Aside from that, my information read that he spent something like three hours a day in church, and almost all the rest of his time with a vodka bottle.

Jimmy Dexter, when I'd talked with him from London on the scrambler phone two days before, had laughed at me and told me I was right. "Of course the fellow isn't worth a nickel."

"Then why do we bother with him? He's not even really a king at all. Just the Rumanian pretender."

"You mean one of the Rumanian pretenders. There's another one, who actually ruled for a few years, until the Russians dumped him, back in '47. His name's Michael and he lives in France somewhere, but we're not interested in him. You see, Steve, he signed a formal Act of Abdication. He renounced it later—almost a year later, long after he and the queen had settled down in exile—but you just don't do that in the king business. Not if you are trying to maintain loyalty, allegiance, and respect among your subjects. And most definitely not when you have competition."

"Who's our man? A younger brother?"

"Now that's a good question. There you've got to bear in mind the circumstances and the personalities involved. Rumania in the twenties was a feudal monarchy. The court of Carol II was dominated by his mother, Queen Marie, who ran the country while he ran a string of playgirls—maybe you'll remember the head bunny's name, Magda Lupescu. She's the one who had a son by him in 1921, in the same week his wife, Queen Helena, gave birth to Michael. There's supposed to be some sort of evidence that the two baby boys were switched, by Queen Marie. Of course it doesn't really matter if they were or not—what matters is that millions of Rumanian peasants think they were."

That, more or less, had satisfied me. Balkan peasants, in large numbers, are a valuable commodity. Rumania has sixteen million of them, held down by four million city slickers who include maybe a hundred thousand half-assed communists. Control the peasantry, and you can pry the country loose, out of the Warsaw Pact, at the right time. Meanwhile you've got both feet right on the edge of Mother Russia's back yard where the fence has no barbed wire in it.

If Carol Rudolph Ferdinand von Hohenzollern-Sigmaringen could deliver this peasantry, it might be useful keeping him in vodka. Yuri Franklin would appreciate that, it had occurred to me when we were introduced. She didn't look to be the lazy type, but most of us enjoy as much time off as we can get.

The royal household's third member was something else again. "Our *chef de cabinet*, Prince Otto Sturza. Mr. Stephen Harvester."

"Good evening, Your Highness."

"Howdedo." Starched British accent, cavalry mustache, cropped bullethead, age over seventy. "You're the American, ah, journalist we've been expecting, are you not."

"That's right, sir."

"Very well. His Majesty will grant you audience sometime next week. You will be notified. You'll have the courtesy not to presume upon us on this social occasion."

I had smiled, not really very courteously, and moved along, and a few minutes later Yuri had caught up with me. "You mustn't be annoyed with the old gentleman."

"I'm an old gentleman myself."

"Uh-uh, you're not. You never will be."

"Now what's that supposed to mean? I'm fifty-four, Miss Franklin. I propose to stay this age for the next thirty years."

"My point exactly. And I'd have believed you if you had said forty-four."

One of the stewards passed us with his trayload of champagne. Marcia Ellis is a DAR, but she believes in British sailors and in British servants. She employs a staff and crew of thirty of them, on her yacht and in her household, and she doesn't go about collecting them. I took two glasses, offered one to Yuri, and took stock of her with more or less professional concern. Young ladies who've gone into business for themselves almost invariably show it. You can get into a serious argument about that in the locker room; they will assure you that all women are for sale, or they'll explain to you that nobody can tell the difference between amateurs and pros, these days. But they're mistaken. Almost always there's a little label somewhere in plain view that says quite clearly *I want to be paid for it.* There's nothing wrong with that, of course—it's only logical and sensible, and will avoid misunderstanding if you're shopping or if, as in my own line of work, a woman's policy and outlook are important when you have to deal with her.

This girl displayed no label. Oriental blood or college education don't much influence these things. Sometimes, of course, a blind spot in the eye of the beholder will occur, but my emotions were in focus elsewhere, and my appetites were reasonably well under control. "You're very kind," I said. "But there's a mirror in the bathroom where I shave."

"Prince Sturza uses one," she told me sweetly. "What he sees in it is Carol's father, fifty years ago, on a white horse. With himself on a black one, just a little bit behind and to the left."

I realized all that, but I was not so sure what she was trying to accomplish.

"Miss Franklin, you're not interested in publicity, are you?"

Her smile was mocking me. "Well, after all, you're certainly attractive. We could use you in the picture layout on His Majesty. We'll have to be a little cagey over what we say about you in the captions, but it never hurts to be in *Esquire* magazine, does it?"

"I'd like that very much," she solemnly assured me. "Only that's not, as we say back home, the name of the game, is it, Steve Harvester?"

My neck had done a quick one-eighty. We were in a corner of the grand salon, and we had doubtful privacy. She knew too much, that was immediately obvious. "His Majesty confides in you, Miss Franklin, does he?"

"Yes, he does. So you might just as well."

"I'm sorry, but that doesn't follow, and I'm not disposed to talk about it here. May I suggest you phone me? At the Rif Hotel."

She laughed her tinkling little laugh as if I'd said something extremely witty, blew a kiss, and slipped away from me. That was two hours ago, before the Strawberry Preserves Conspiracy had been announced.

The fountain in the garden giggled quietly to itself as it had done for more than eighteen hundred years. Perhaps the sound ought to have helped me concentrate. But it succeeded only in evoking what amounted to a sense of philosophical futility. In eighteen centuries, how many like myself had sat here, and had listened to it, wishing it would solve a problem, restore youth, summon a lover, drown an enemy? The quandary at hand was really not all that intractable. Since Carol Rudolf Ferdinand the Third had proven himself indiscreet, I could advise New York that we abandon him.

Or I could take a closer look. There was no hurry. Not as far as I could see.

Footsteps crunched on the graveled walk from the direction of the house. The fruity, heavily accented tenor of Leon de Bas addressed me from the shadows of an ancient cypress. "Mister 'Arvestair! Ah, there you are. Our hostess has commanded me to bring you back to her."

"Has she?"

"It seems our talented young visitors from the United States have not yet seen a belly dancer. Naturally such improvidence must be at once corrected."

"Naturally."

"You and I have been appointed to be their escort. So have Mr. Wahlstrom and Miss Franklin and, of course, Madame Ellis herself."

Marcia's peculiar sense of humor does run to this kind of exercise. I wasn't in the mood for it, or in the mood for arguing with her. I started asking de Bas not to tell her that he'd found me, but he put me off; he had begun to make a noise that sounded like he'd turned a fire hose on the cypress. "What the devil are you doing?"

"Making water, my dear fellow. It's that fountain. Don't you find that it induces one to emulate it?"

Some of us have halitosis, but this seemed a good deal worse. I hurried out of range and strode back to the house without another word. The expedition was assembling in the courtyard, boarding one of Marcia's Eldorados and the Strawberry Preserves Conspiracy's decrepit Volkswagen, whose bumper stickers wanted us to grant AMNESTY NOW and to DUCK DIRTY DICK. De Bas came waddling after me and crowded in with me into the front seat of the Caddie. The starched British chauffeur slammed the door on him. "El Djinn, please," ordered Marcia, regally installed in the tonneau with Wahlstrom and the Franklin hussy in attendance. "Take it easy, will you, Geoffrey? Let those kids stay with you."

"Very good, madam."

We coasted down toward the city, with the dazzle-painted

minibus groaning in close pursuit. Ten minutes with Leon de
Bas beside me, even in an air-conditioned car, was long
enough, but he seemed sociably unaware of it while he kept up
a running commentary on the minor curiosities of Tangier traffic: strolling Arab men, in European dress but holding hands;
veiled Arab girls riding French racing bikes; and the unceasing
menace of Moroccan truck drivers, their smoking junk heaps
charging past us, each one with a helper on the tailgate to
ward off the evil spirits that might reasonably be assumed to
follow them.

The Kasbah clings to a steep hill that overlooks the port. Its
principal components are a lot of filthy plaster walls and dung-
packed, cobblestone-paved alleys, some of them degenerating
into tunnels. Nothing bigger than a donkey cart can move
around in it; your milkman, if you live there, is a goat herd,
and there are no sewers, street lights, firemen, garbage men, or
cops on regular patrol. Yet there are some luxurious residences
in there, and a sultan's palace, and there are expensive shops
and restaurants, and nightclubs. Geoffrey parked by the Bastinado Gate where minor wrongdoers used to receive their just
reward, in public, on the soles of their feet. He came up with a
flashlight from the glove compartment, disembarked us, locked
the car, and watched the minibus with critical disdain as it
pulled in behind us and disgorged its occupants. Then he
walked through the gate, preceding us, and led us off into the
maze.

A party of ten Europeans, half of them in dinner dress,
might have stirred up considerable turmoil earlier in the evening. But it was after hours for the pros, the men with the ar-
tistic mutilations, and the scabrous women with the rented
babies; only a small pack of little boys snapped at our heels,
their skulls shaved bare but for the customary top knot by
which Allah might, if so disposed, jerk them up into heaven.
Here and there a burning coach lamp marked the doorways

that were still expecting visitors. El Djinn's seemed to be one of these but was not otherwise identified. I knew the place by reputation only, but the chauffeur guided us to it without the slightest difficulty.

"Shall I wait here for you, madam?"

"No, no, no. Do join us, Geoffrey. Help us watch the children."

This appeared to be a sensible idea. The Strawberry Preserves Conspiracy had lagged behind. Some fifty feet away, its members crowded in the light of an acetylene lantern that shone down on the body of a man reclining on the pavement. Geoffrey raised an eyebrow at me and I shrugged, walked back with him, and joined the group. The Arab on the cobblestones lay moaning but seemed not to be in serious distress; a second Arab, grizzle-bearded, wizened with old age, had pushed down his djellaba to the waist and squatted by his side watching intently as he placed a bright green lizard on the prone man's stomach. The small animal relaxed immediately and fixed its beady little eyes on him. A pulse beat fluttered visibly in the protuberance under its throat. It started to change color, to a mottled pink.

The girl said: "Wow, what's happening?" Her three associates merely stared. I'd casually met them after dinner, by what they were using for first names—the girl was Val, her boyfriend with the handlebar mustache called himself Mick. The black boy wanted to be known as Hero Pud; the precious blondie seemed to be content with Croup. "You're looking at a sidewalk doctor and his patient," I said pleasantly enough. "That's a chameleon lizard. It's supposed to diagnose diseases by the color it assumes."

"No shit," said Hero Pud, straight faced. "Hey, that's far out, man, that's for me. This cat on Blue Cross or American Express?"

"Let's move along," I said. "If you were sick you wouldn't

like a bunch of tourists rubbernecking. If you were the hostess, you wouldn't like waiting for your guests."

That earned me the full concert of their flat-eyed stares. "Hey man, who you to put us down?" demanded Mick. "We figured you were with it."

He could only mean one thing. Except during my four years in the air force, I have always worn my hair down to the collar line; and it is black without much frost to it, if you don't come too close. "You goofed, man, I'm the enemy."

"No shit."

"So let's move out."

They did, with evident reluctance. The chauffeur, Geoffrey, closed ranks behind them, glancing at me from the corner of one jaundiced eye. We were admitted to the portals of El Djinn by what could only be the bouncer, an enormous Moor in a red fez and pantaloons, bare arms and chest bloated with muscle, who took notice of our protégés with a profound and obvious disdain. Inside, the other members of our party were already being seated on the usual low taborets at a round table board of heavy oak and cocktail height.

The room was sizable, low-ceilinged, and partitioned by tall screens of fretted tile. It probably was very old and not particularly clean. But it was making money. That much could be sensed immediately from the noise alone. Ear plugs would have been very useful, and an oxygen mask, and a double Scotch. Available were mint tea, almond cakes, and Turkish coffee or, as a concession to the tourist trade, straight Coca-Cola from the bottle, warm, the saucers price-marked, in the manner of French sidewalk cafés, at ten dirhams each—about two dollars. I found myself on Marcia's left, and wedged in close between her and the kid with the Mongolian mustache and the Irish name. The table made a tight fit for the ten of us, with little leg room, practically forcing us to stick our feet out under it.

"Hey, man, we heard that the old lady has a boat like the *Queen Mary*. That for real?"

"It's a converted navy frigate," I said coldly. "They're not very big or fast, but this one has been worked on. It can make it to New York from here in four, five days."

"That's where we're going, man. Big Barnsmell on the Hudson. Think she'd take us?"

I looked at him carefully. He couldn't be much over twenty. He was not exactly rose-lipped, or still wet behind the ears, but if you were a bartender you'd ask for his i.d. "As far as I know, Mrs. Ellis hasn't visited New York in years," I said.

He winked for me, a randy wink, junior satyr style, and pointed with his chin. Marcia was talking briskly to his girl friend, Val, whom she'd inserted on her right. I shrugged and scanned the others: Captain Wahlstrom, next in line, looked courteously bored. The black kid, Hero Pud, was yawning openly; the British chauffeur, deadpan, sipped his tea. The blond boy, Croup, seemed to be lecturing Leon de Bas, who listened gravely, purse-mouthed, squeezing out the fleshy promontory of his chin.

Miss Yuri Franklin bestowed a tantalizing smile on Mick. "How'd you guys happen to meet Mrs. Ellis Mick?" she inquired.

"We heard about her," he said vaguely.

I was pretty sure of that. The word on Marcia had gone out quite a long time ago. She was supposed to be the ripest—walk right up to her and ask for it. Of course she's not like that at all. She's like a fisher-woman who believes in using chum.

The belly dancer came under that category, I suspected. She appeared within five minutes after we got settled down. They didn't want to keep you in suspense in there—they wanted you to have what you came in for and be on your way, or buy another Coke and see another show. They must have had at least three girls, because there were two working all the time, behind the tile screens separating us from other tables, with the orchestra supplying a sustained accompaniment, gourds and bagpipes only, fast, and reedily insistent, but not very loud.

The girl assigned to us just walked right in and jumped up on our table, smiling sweetly, draped from neck to toe in a loose yellow caftan. She was young and pretty, with a sky-blue tribal mark and quite a lot of kohl and rouge for makeup, skillfully applied. Her hair had been piled high and brought under severe control with crisscrossed silver clamps. She dropped the caftan, kicked it into Wahlstrom's face, and went into her act.

She was completely nude, of course, and shaved, and rouged judiciously. There's no comparison, not even a remote one, between what these girls perform and anything you ever saw done in Istanbul or Tahiti, or behind a bar counter in Cicero. There is a common low denominator, since all human females dance to invite copulation and to imitate same, but these Berber women must be seen to be believed.

The temperature at our table went up at least twenty degrees Fahrenheit in sixty seconds. Even Marcia started reaching for the Kleenex in her purse. Wahlstrom's ennui had dissipated in a hurry—he still clutched the dancer's garment as he watched, his monocle dangling forgotten, his aristocratic hatchet face flushed pink. The chauffeur, Geoffrey, sat up rigidly, licking his lips; Leon de Bas was scowling openly, a scowl of fascination with the odious, the insufferable. Yuri Franklin caught my eye and shivered visibly, half-pleasurably, as though she were well aware of my own primitive reaction.

The Strawberry Preserves Conspiracy showed a collective, open-mouthed bewilderment.

When it was over and the dancer, laughing at us, had snatched back her caftan and run off with it, they were the only ones to break into delayed applause. Mick slapped my shoulder. "Wow, man! Outasite!"

"Yay, she's a trip!" the black kid, Hero Pud, concurred with him. "Like wet 'n' wild, man. Like you never saw."

The blondie, Croup, with a quick sidelong glance directed at Leon de Bas, said thoughtfully: "She's dynamite, all right.

She'd, like, you know, trash you to little pieces if you tried to make it with her."

Hero Pud blew him a careless raspberry. Marcia, with one possessive arm around Mick's girl friend's shoulder, asked her: "Did you dig it, sweetie?"

"Wow, yeah! I sure did."

She sounded more bemused than persuaded. Waiters were already swarming in, intent on either selling us another round or ushering us out. Marcia put money on the table, rose, and brought us to our feet. The sidewalk doctor under the acetylene lantern had disappeared; the alley leading to the Bastinado Gate looked even less salubrious than it had before. The chauffeur's flashlight guided us around the donkey droppings and across the open gutters that seemed somehow preferable to the clogging atmosphere of body smells and kif smoke at El Djinn's.

When I dropped back a little, making sure we wouldn't lose the kids again, Sven Wahlstrom joined me, monocle inserted resolutely in its proper place again. "A sordid business."

"Yes, you could say that, I suppose."

He came down to a murmur. "You assure me that your, ah, organization isn't interested in de Bas?"

"We may be. All I told you was that I'm not now concerned with him."

"Or with this Operation Dancing Dog?"

"That's right."

He shook his head and moved away from me. Our party filed out through the gate and found its transportation. From the windshield wiper of the psychedelically painted minibus fluttered a parking ticket, but the Eldorado next to it apparently had not been noticed by the cops. AMNESTY NOW. DUCK DIRTY DICK. The chauffeur, Geoffrey, took the ticket, glanced at Marcia, and put it in his pocket. He embarked us, slid behind the wheel, and sent the Caddie whispering uphill.

TANGIER, SATURDAY, JULY 17.

The lobby of the Rif Hotel at two A.M. was adequately busy. The location is about the best in town, for tourists—on the beach and near the port—and the accommodations are as good as anything in Africa. They keep three bars open as long as there are customers, and the last cabaret show is at one o'clock. They have a belly dancer you could take your maiden aunt to see; indeed, she easily might be your maiden aunt.

The porter's desk supplied a message slip when I picked up my key. One glance at it bounced up my pulse rate, pleasurably but alarmingly. It seemed to take me a long time to reach my room and get the phone up to my ear. Long-distance operators in Morocco and in Spain are marvels of efficiency, if you speak Spanish. I was through in forty seconds by my watch, across the Strait and sixty miles along the coast. Not bad at all, if there'd been any way to make the sweep hand on the dial move. *"Muy buenas, Señor Harvester. Lo siento mucho, la señora duerme."* It was Lita's butler-chauffeur-bodyguard, a sergeant-major in the army of Colombia, informing me that she'd retired.

She'd arrived early, two weeks early. It had never happened before, but there'd be a reason, and she'd almost certainly have cabled me in London, missing me by a few hours. Tracing me here to the Rif must have been simple. There's a twenty-four-hour service on my private phone that rarely gets instructions to play dumb. A writer has to keep in touch.

I told Jacinto I'd be over on the hydrofoil that afternoon, and he politely thanked me and hung up, the merest fraction of a moment faster than he should have if he'd judged me worthy of respect. I listened carefully for just that tiny breach in courtesy. It was of cardinal importance, and its failure to occur would indicate the most disastrous possibilities. But it was there, and I breathed easier, and started to prepare for bed. There was no way of traveling to Spain within the next twelve hours except by chartered plane or launch. Paid fancy men don't charter transportation. Lovers do, when able to afford it, but a lover to Señora Doña Isabella Luz de Vargas I was definitely not supposed to be.

You learn to cope with your uncomfortable thoughts, your troublesome emotions. Or you take the tranquilizer route and come to disrespect yourself. I'd managed to stay clear of that one, mostly. That night I made do with a short Scotch in Vichy water and a tepid shower. It took concentration, but ten minutes on the pillow put me off to sleep.

Hotel thieves and assistant managers know how to bypass door chains, which are useful only to keep out the amateurs and to announce that you are in your room. This time a little noise was made, perhaps not unintentionally. It was just enough to waken me and get me to the bathroom with a gun. The bedroom ceiling light came on, which meant that they were cops. I pushed the little Airweight Cobra between towels on the rack, and flushed the toilet, and walked out behind a credible expression of hurt dignity.

The two in khaki and white helmets were the usual patrolman team, a tough old Arab and a cocky young one, French-trained for insensitivity. The little man in the civilian ice-cream suit looked French himself, but on the card he handed me his name was Hamid Aziz, Inspecteur, Brigade Criminelle de la Police Municipale de Tanger. He spoke fractured English with a Dixie drawl; he must have worked for somebody in CIC or CID during War Two, in Casablanca. It could even have been me. I had a Texas accent in those days.

"What y'all be inna john for, mistah?"

"You've got ears," I said. "What's on your mind, inspector? How did you get in?"

He jerked his head at the patrolmen, and the young one kicked the bathroom door I'd left ajar, and wandered through. He yanked the shower curtain, wandered back again, and shrugged. I managed easily not to look worried. They can cut your head off for possession of a gun in Africa, but it's more customary for a little money to change hands. Such as ten dollars to the lucky officer, fifteen if there are two or three. Inspector Aziz kept his beady eye on me while I sat down and lit a cigarette. "Y'all not expectin' visitahs, mistah?"

"This time of night?"

My watch was on the bedside table, out of sight, but I was sure I'd slept less than an hour; the smoky Scotch tang lingered on my palate. "Yessah, mistah," said Aziz. "Y'all not expectin' visitahs. Tell operatah, no disturb." He snickered for my benefit, conspiratorially, as if I'd had a shrewd idea with interesting sexual implications he could thoroughly appreciate. He casually opened the big wardrobe doors and glanced inside.

I shook my head and told him I had left no such instructions with the operator. But he visibly did not believe me. "Is a shame, mistah. Concierge turn back yo' frien'. Or he still be alive, no?" When he saw I wasn't going to look guilty or surprised he finally came round to asking what he had to ask. "What Mistah Wahlstrom want with y'all?"

In thirty years I still hadn't got used to it. I'd killed about three dozen people, seven of them face to face, the rest by more or less remote control. I'd witnessed executions, fatal accidents, and terminal disease, not quite as many cases as a doctor or the average policeman sees, but certainly enough of them. You're not supposed to like it, or to become hardened by it, but you are supposed to make what the psychologists call an adjustment. All I had been able to achieve was a facsimile of this, and not a very reasonable one.

"I know Count Wahlstrom socially," I said. "You're telling me he's dead?" Aziz just looked at me. The old Arab patrolman spat into my wastebasket, politely. "If he came to see me, I have no idea what it could be about, inspector. We were at a dinner party earlier this evening—last night. Our conversation was entirely without substance, trivial. What happened to him?"

The Moroccan crooked a finger at me. He was opening the French doors, letting in the sultry night air with the lisp of distant surf, the sudden stridor of a passing car on Avenue d'Espagne. The air-conditioner, its thermostat insulted, promptly racketed back into action. I got up and joined him on the balcony. The ambulance had left already, but it hadn't done much of a job of cleaning up after itself. The floodlight on the roof of the investigation van revealed this all too hideously. It also showed the usual chalk outline on the pavement of the avenue.

"Hit-run," I said, not really managing a questioning inflection. It was obviously murder. Wahlstrom was athletic, young, and hadn't had a single drink all evening, not in my sight. "No witnesses?"

"Sure, mistah, we got witnesses," Aziz assured me. "Also we got that." He actually pronounced it *tha-yut*, as I used to, many years ago, for emphasis. He pointed off toward the left. A truck of sorts, an ancient four-by-four, had slammed into a palm tree fifty yards away. A wrecker was already fussing with it, getting ready to hook onto it. Two motor cops stood by on widespread legs, heroically posed, their cycles kick-standed behind them on the sidewalk. It was clear immediately what had happened—they'd arrived, by a remarkable coincidence, in time to twist their handlebars and cut the truck into the tree.

"The driver?"

"Break his neck, mistah. We know him." Meaning that he had a record, probably including at least one other pedestrian collision, fatal. With a helper on the tailgate who'd be either very young or very old, retarded or senile. But I was not supposed to ask, or even guess, or mention that the Avenue d'Espagne was not a normal route for trucks. "Y'all tell me now what Mistah Wahlstrom want with y'all?"

"I've told you about that, inspector. I don't know."

"Why y'all tell operatah, no disturb?"

"I didn't. Maybe she misunderstood."

He sadly shook his head and motioned me into the room. He closed the balcony doors very carefully, as if they were his private property. "Mistah, I got some news fo' y'all."

"Do you?"

"Las' night, comes phone call to police. It say that y'all and Mistah Wahlstrom have bad quarrel about woman."

"Oh? Did it say which woman?"

"Sure, mistah, you know tha-yut." He was visibly and audibly deploring my naïveté.

I couldn't think of any better way to keep him off my back. A flat denial was what he'd expect if I were guilty. Innocence, according to his lights, would be revealed either by serious concern and an immediate offer to cooperate, or by impertinence, an attitude of childish nonchalance, a jet-set attitude. I wasn't very interested in cooperating with him, and still less in letting him discover just how nonchalant I might or might not be.

He made his mind up, jerked a thumb at the patrolmen and the door, and told me not to leave Tangier without permission from the *juge d'instruction*, the magistrate in charge of criminal investigations. I objected promptly, with a show of arrogance. "Who needs permission? I am not a witness in this matter. I intend to go to Spain this afternoon and to return next week. If you propose to stop me, I shall telephone my consul right away, this minute."

"Mistah, y'all don' understan'. We wish to learn why Mistah Wahlstrom come to visit y'all."

"That's fine," I said. "When you find out, you let me know. Now here's what *you* don't understand, inspector. I'm a journalist. There are some forty million people in America who read the magazines I work for. Do you follow me?" He sneered at me, and I picked up the phone. He stopped me with a hand wave and a shrug, and walked out of the room.

I sat down on the bed. I could have used a drink, but if you pamper yourself every time there's a problem, the insurance companies won't make a profit on you. As it was, the problem didn't strike me as particularly bothersome. Wahlstrom, quite evidently, had been mouse-trapped. Something of an effort had been made to pull me in—I had no doubt that the same telephone voice that had tipped off the police had also summoned Wahlstrom to a meeting with me at the Rif Hotel. The voice had probably been female, but the only reasonable instigator I could see behind it was Leon de Bas.

That was all right. I wasn't going to do anything about it, and I didn't even blame the man; he was just trying to defend himself. He'd come to the entirely justifiable conclusion that this NATO officer was here to set him up, not to negotiate with him. I wasn't NATO, but it looked like I was helping out, so it made sense to take a crack at me as well. There was no point in troubling to return the compliment. Brussels would send three men, or half a dozen, in a day or two. I hooked the useless door chain up again, retrieved my pistol from the towel rack, and went right back to sleep.

Miss Yuri Franklin called at breakfast time. The elderly French waiter who was serving mine cocked a brash ear and a sardonic eyebrow at my segment of the conversation. "Hello,

good morning. . . . Of course I am. Are you? . . . Yes, I did
suggest we get together. I'm not sure about this weekend, but
by Monday night or Tuesday afternoon. . . . Oh. You're in
the lobby now. Well, fine! If you'll excuse my informality,
Miss Franklin . . . Okay, come right on up." The waiter
dawdled long enough to let her in. She wore a minishift of
starched white linen and a cleverly designed mock-adaptation
of the Arab haik, the women's headgear that hides everything
except the eyes but that could be reorganized, in her case, by a
slight adjustment of the neck. Its contrast to the yard of shapely legs she had on view was nothing less than persuasive.
"Well, hello again! I certainly appreciate this. How d'you
manage to look tantalizing at this hour of the morning?"

"It is very difficult, Steve Harvester. I had to force myself."

"I see."

She asked for coffee and croissants. The waiter didn't run to
bring them, but he wanted to. When he returned he found us
on the balcony, watching the early water skiers. On the Avenue d'Espagne no traces of the night's brutality remained. I
didn't mention it to her—when she'd been served, and we had
privacy, it seemed much better to come to the point immediately. "The subject for discussion between us is confidence, Miss
Franklin, isn't it?"

"Yes, I suppose so."

"Last night you implied that you'd been told about the
background reason for my article about His Majesty. Will you
explain that, please?"

She had removed the veil and was enjoying half a croissant
dripping with marmalade. Most women would have had problems, but she managed to make quite a sensual production out
of it. "Do you want me to explain how I've won Carol's confidence?" she asked.

"I'm interested in that, too. But only socially. It worries me
a little that you're fencing with me."

"But I'm not. Look, I'm as much concerned as you are about Carol's future. More than you are, because after all he doesn't really mean much to you. You're only trying to coordinate his followers through him."

"And you, Miss Franklin? What exactly are you trying to coordinate?"

She laughed at me, of course. Most girls sound artificial, tinkling like a little silver bell, but she came on sincere, somehow. "You won't believe me if I tell you that he swept me off my feet, will you."

"It seems unlikely."

"Well, he drinks a lot, but he's not bad, you know. You must've heard he goes for the religious bit. He has a private chaplain, all that sort of thing, only that's mostly just pretend. The folks back home in Bukowina are the orthodox type, and they like to hear that he is with it." She turned on a cool and level stare for me. "Do you have information about me, Steve Harvester?"

"There is a file on you. There's one on everybody in the world."

She shrugged it off. She had admitted that she wanted money, almost in so many words. Even a Stanford graduate in anthropology needs money. That could be arranged, if she'd give value in return. "Let's get this straight," I said. "You were let in on something confidential. I'm not sure just how my people will react—it's possible that they'll instruct me to walk out. They will unless I tell them that I think we can do business with you. You're an American, but that's not good enough these days. They'll ask me to appraise your loyalty. If it's for sale, I'll have to estimate whether it'll stay bought."

"Which means you'll have to get to know me, doesn't it."

There was no laughing at me now. She was dead-serious, as a professional at the negotiating table has to be. I shrugged and said: "Not necessarily, Miss Franklin."

"Oh, you mean your people may not care to take a chance. I shouldn't have talked out of turn to you last night. But you'd 've found out later anyway. That's why I did." She lay back on the chaise longue and crossed her pretty legs, and studied me to see how she was coming over. She was doing fine—I could believe her. It was just the sort of calculated indiscretion that scores points for your side if you handle yourself well.

Of course I wasn't going to call Jimmy Dexter. He'd just tell me to evaluate the situation for myself and recommend accordingly.

There would be time enough for that: a week or two, a month if need be. Carol Rudolf Ferdinand the Third could wait. He wasn't broke yet, just insolvent. Royalty, even Balkan royalty in exile, usually manage to run up quite a lot of tradesman's bills.

Meanwhile there was this problem child on my chaise longue.

I didn't mind particularly if she ever talked. Moscow would hear about our friendly little back yard intrigue soon enough, but the mere knowledge of it would be useless. There was nothing sensible that could be done about it. Drastic stuff would only play into our hands. Outbidding us would be as feasible as buying off a cock from treading hens: he knows already that he's wanted in the pot, not in the roost. Denouncing us and trying for a propaganda victory would require evidence, and that we certainly did not intend to make available. The unsupported tattle of a concubine could hardly qualify as evidence.

But she could hurt us if she tried. Women can be just as pragmatic about paid-for loyalty as men, and just as capable of it; the only risk lies in a sudden change in their emotional allegiance. Men can be seduced and tapped for information, but unless he is a homosexual it's very difficult to turn a man around that way and make him work for you. A woman, if you get to her, will go the route.

Miss Yuri Franklin looked to me as near seduction-proof as anything on hand.

I had the notion that, instinctively or otherwise, she wanted me to be aware of it. There is a kind of female sexuality best characterized as cool cookie. When this manifests itself in high school girls it's rarely more than make-believe, but over twenty and in trade has very little need to put you on. The lady in the starched white minishift was decorously posing and demurely smiling. Nothing she had said or done could reasonably be mistaken for an invitation. Having breakfast with a man wearing pajama bottoms and a dressing gown apparently held no significance for her at all. Yet it was obvious indeed that I could help myself to her, if so inclined, and that no obligations other than those normally incurred when sampling merchandise would fall on me or, for that matter, on her.

Even at fifty-four I was as much susceptible in the department of biology as any other male. Age and experience only served as power brakes, to be applied or not. I carefully applied them, looked at her across my coffee cup, and said: "Assume we try to come to terms with you, Miss Franklin, would you like to give me an idea of your financial requirements?"

"For not talking out of turn again? I couldn't expect money for that, could I?"

"Ethically speaking, no."

"But your organization is prepared to, well, support my ethics."

"Maybe so. I'm pretty sure we'd go for just a little more. We'd want you to think highly of us, and to influence His Majesty accordingly. We might even suggest that if you came across the sort of information we'd be interested in, you'd find a way of passing it along to us."

She nodded, smiling almost dewily. "I have a bank account in Zürich. Would five thousand francs a month be fair?"

"Swiss francs? Don't you believe in dollars?"

"There's no gold revaluation problem or unfavorable trade balance in Switzerland."

"Only because we keep the Russians off their back. But what you're asking for is in the ball park. Why don't I propose it to New York on your behalf, Miss Franklin? You might carry on for a few days while they consider it."

"All right, I will." She moved one leg, enough to give me reason to believe her pantyhose were sheer all the way up. "Wasn't that dancer at El Djinn last night too much?"

"She made me totter with the burden of my years," I said.

The misty smile became a shade less innocent. "You're an amusing fraud, Steve Harvester. But not a very enterprising one."

"That's true enough."

"Shall I tell Carol that I made a pass at you to feel you out, but that you were a perfect gentleman? He loves that sort of thing."

"Yes, by all means."

This time she laughed with me. She rose, affixed the veil in place, came over to me, stood on tiptoes, looked up in my eyes, and quite deliberately, expertly, made body contact with me. " . . . You're not so perfect."

"I'm afraid you're right."

"And I'm a cruel bitch." She bit my neck, not very hard, and twisted out of reach, and slipped out of the room.

Leon de Bas walked in shortly after eleven-thirty, with a pass key he'd have bought or borrowed from the maid. He caught me packing, and bestowed a vast and knowing smirk on me. "Off for the weekend, my dear fellow?" He sat down on the small taboret provided for a woman guest using the vanity. It creaked disturbingly under his weight.

I stared at him, my hands filled with assorted toilet articles.

He was supposed to be as dangerous as a wild buffalo, but all I saw was an obese old man in high-rise doeskin slacks over a sportshirt of fine cambric with a floral print. The juicy Gallic accent and the slightly precious turn of phrase continued to annoy me. "Something I can do for you?"

"There is, my boy. Most certainly there is."

I went on with my packing and ignored him while he watched and squeezed his triple chins. After a while he spoke up querulously. "You seem, ah, disinterested, 'Arvestair."

"Correct."

"But we have much in common. We must reach a meeting of the minds."

"Must we?"

"You are a writer," he reminded me. "Perhaps not of a caliber for the Académie Française or for the Prix Nobel, but passable. I am familiar with your work, my boy, and I've enjoyed it. I respect your talent, your philosophy, the influence you exercise over your readers. It is a shame that you neglect these things, wasting yourself and your invaluable time."

"Stop sounding like my publishers," I said. "You'll make me cry."

"No, no, this is no joking matter, please. You do misspend yourself, most frightfully, I'm sure you realize that, 'Arvestair. There was a time when the profession of intelligence could be considered honorable and important, but that has not been the case for many years, of course. There are so very many of us now that we've degraded ourselves, vulgarized ourselves. We're little more than garbage men. Less, actually, since they have a useful function. We do not, not anymore."

"You think so?"

"Come now, my dear fellow. It was long ago, you must admit. We were expected to discover secrets or to guard them, as the case might be—it was our *raison d'être*, the sole purpose of our trade. But then what happened? Well before your time and mine this core of ours had started to decay. We fed upon it, consumed it, destroyed it as though we were termites ruining the house that sheltered us. The principle of secrecy itself has virtually ceased to exist." He watched me close and lock my bags and put them on the luggage rack, ready to be collected by the porter. "You're not leaving yet, are you, my boy?"

"What do you care, de Bas?" I asked him cheerfully. "You just explained that we're all through."

"Forgive me, but I did not quite say that. There are still a few secrets, as you know. They really don't deserve the name, since they cannot be kept, at least not very long—they have a half-life, like unstable elements, that lasts for a few weeks or so. We dabble in them, shift them like a dozen peas under a hundred walnut shells, but we are actually not too much concerned with them. Instead, we seem to be reduced to brawling with each other. Vulgarly. Degradingly."

"Sounds like you're ready to retire," I said.

"No, no, not I. You, my dear 'Arvestair. You are in this for pay and, possibly, for so-called patriotic reasons. But you can make money with your typewriter and, as you're very well aware, patriotism has expired. The current generation does not even recognize the word."

I listened to him with one ear, using the other on the phone. The porter's desk was busy. "So what's your excuse for staying in?" I asked de Bas. "You're not exactly broke."

His manicure was occupying his attention. He was studying it like a woman, palms up first, with fingers bent, to see the angle of the nails on view to others; then palms down, fingers extended, for the angle in perspective to himself. The varnish was a salmon pink with orange overtones. "You startle me, my boy. Haven't you done your homework on me?"

"What there was of it."

"Then you should know that I am worth perhaps ten million dollars. All of it sequestered, confiscated, blocked in what is called Kinshasa now but used to be the Belgian Congo. I am a revanchist, 'Arvestair. Not just because of that."

The desk came on and promised me a porter. I hung up and sat down on the bed. "All right," I said. "You're a revanchist. You don't like what happened in the Congo, ten-twelve years ago. You lost your money, and some native drunks got to your sister, so you met somebody in the KGB and volunteered. That makes good sense."

He didn't glare at me. His bland, perspiring moonface hardly changed expression. But the malice flowed from him so strongly I could lean on it. I had been into Léopoldville and Elisabethville a few times myself, in '60 and in '62, and I'd been lucky to come out with nothing but a lot of nightmares. The United Nations had come hopelessly balls up on it, I was convinced of that. Washington had been sitting on its hands, but it had managed somehow to make everybody think that it was after the uranium.

"Not native drunks," de Bas said. "Indian drunks. Madrassi troopers from the U.N. forces in Katanga. Six of them."

"Moscow's a member," I reminded him.

"You don't believe that, my dear fellow."

He was scoffing at me, not entirely without reason. "Fair enough," I said. "And since we're being frank, maybe you'd like to tell me why you shut off Captain Wahlstrom. It's no skin off my back, but the boys at Section Six won't be particularly pleased with you when they find out. Which should be about now." My watch said 12:05. I'd planned a leisurely second breakfast on the terrace before catching the Marbella hydrofoil at two P.M. The porter knocked, entered, salaamed, and took my bags. When I looked at de Bas again, he had not moved an inch.

His stare at me had a peculiar quality of petulance mixed with distrust. "I have been told there was a traffic accident," he said impassively.

"Who told you that?"

He raised both hands, annoyed with me. "Spare me your levity, please, 'Arvestair. As is the case with all of us, I am quite capable of organizing violence. If necessary, I shall do so to prevent you from corrupting these lamentable Rumanians. Is that understood?"

"Go on."

"I did not kill young Wahlstrom. I have been negotiating with him. About delicate and personal affairs."

"Well, very good," I said. "It's taken you a little time, but now we've got around to why you're here. You want me to stop doing business with the Rumanians, and you'd like me to do business with you. On Dancing Dog, of course."

There was no hope of getting him to show surprise; he merely squatted on his creaking little taboret and squeezed his · chins. He wasn't even looking at me anymore. "In touch with Brussels, are you, my dear fellow."

"Draw your own conclusions."

"Then you know I had no reason to touch Wahlstrom. We were making progress. His misfortune inconveniences me."

"He did recommend Section Six going along with you," I said. "This traffic accident'll put them off."

"I doubt it," he said placidly. "They'll ask for the police report, and it will satisfy them."

But it was too obvious that he knew better. "They'll ask me," I said. "Now look, de Bas, let's get this straight. You have a problem with your family. You want to go to Belgium for a little while, to deal with it. That means you have to bargain for immunity. You seem to have persuaded Wahlstrom that you had something, but I don't know. This Dancing Dog of yours sounds like a circus act to me." He watched me take my raincoat, typewriter, and briefcase from the closet, but he made no move. "You want to stay and occupy this room, you'd better register," I prompted him.

De Bas said coldly: "Dancing Dog is the development and

the rehearsal of a conduit into the United States. This operation will commence in a few days, and can be checked out and foreclosed while I am still available in Belgium. If we come to terms."

"What will be carried in this conduit?" He ignored that with a shrug; he had already come out with a great deal more than he'd disclosed to Wahlstrom. I had no intention of believing or assisting him, but if he happened to be entering his second childhood with the notion that they would play ball with him in Brussels, I was certainly prepared to cheer him on. "All right, I'll take it up with Section Six, first thing on Monday morning. Something probably can be arranged, if you've got merchandise as good as that on hand."

"How very kind of you, my boy."

The phone rang. On my way to pick it up I glanced at him over my shoulder. He did not exactly sound or look sarcastic, but he had something in mind. I told the phone my name and heard Marcia Ellis's executive soprano. "Steve, please come to lunch."

"I'm going to Marbella for the weekend."

"Oh. How wonderful! She arrived early, did she?"

"Yes, that's right."

"You're not alone," Marcia shrewdly diagnosed. "You're talking business. Steve, be a love, dear, do drop by before you go. I want you to advise me about something that's come up."

"Couldn't it wait?"

"No, dear, it's urgent. Listen, I'll have Captain Harvey run you over if you miss that stupid hydrofoil."

Marcia isn't particularly thrifty, but it wouldn't normally occur to her to waste about a thousand dollars. I controlled my eyebrows, since de Bas was watching them, and told her I'd be right along. The portly Belgian cleared his throat while I hung up, and offered me the contents of his crocodile cigar case. When I waved him off impatiently he helped himself, clipping the butt of the Romeo y Julieta with his eyeteeth and depositing the refuse in an ashtray on the vanity. "There is, of course, the question of my personal security," he said.

"There is?"

"Oh, come now, 'Arvestair. Surely you don't expect me to rely on *words*. Yours, or anyone's in Section Six."

"Frankly, I don't expect a thing from you, de Bas," I said. "If you're afraid of Brussels double-crossing you, I would suggest that you forget about the deal. Now, if you'll please excuse me, I'm a little pressed for time."

He sat there as if it would take a fork lift to remove him. "My dear fellow, you don't seem to understand. I'm offering you and your NATO friends a crucial intelligence coup for a trifling compensation. They will undertake to let me enter Belgium and reside there unmolested for two weeks. You will provide concrete assurance of their bona fides—and of yours."

I didn't laugh. "You mean you want me to put up a bond, here in Tangier? How much, and in which bank?"

"No, no. Money is just a figure on a scrap of paper." He was visibly deploring my simplicity. "Brussels could reimburse you, if they chose to do so, or they could dismiss the matter from their minds. I own a small châlet up in the mountains above Tetuan. It is not quite as comfortable as the beach house of Señora Vargas in Marbella, but I'm sure that for two weeks you can prevail on her to share it with you as my guests."

This time I laughed, not very merrily. "Get out of here before I knock your ears off."

"But why should you?" he demanded, reasonably. He seemed puzzled about such a possibility even presenting itself to me. "There is no offense intended to the lady, and according to my information she has only an *affaire de convenance* with you."

"I don't care to go into that," I said. "I see your point, however, and I'm willing to consider it. If Brussels gives the go-ahead on Monday. Let me have your phone."

He lumbered to his feet and handed me his card which called him *Apex Ingénieurs S.A.* with an address on Rue Pasteur. He was a year older than I, but he looked over seventy just then, and it appeared his kidneys were disturbing him again—he waddled off into the bathroom without bothering to ask permission. I picked up my stuff and walked right out on him. He hadn't put me off that much; I had some pretty good ideas on how to crack the situation, but I was a little tired of him and anxious to be on my way. The porter and the doorman had a taxi waiting with my bags aboard. It dropped me into Marcia's courtyard at 12:37. I was definitely late. Moroccan customs and police believe in fussing over exit passengers.

She met me in the hall under a fourteenth-century mosaic of Saladdin accepting the surrender of the Templar knights. Her kiss was not exactly motherly, but I was not supposed to get any ideas from it. Arms linked, she marched me to the terrace, sat me down behind a bowl of vichyssoise, and smiled on me, conspiratorially. Her English butler brought his sherry cart around. I shook my head, and he urbanely inclined his and went away.

"Is this about Sven Wahlstrom?"

"No, dear. Should it be? You seem surprised."

"You're a big girl now, Marcia," I said. "So take it as it comes. Sven was run over by a truck last night. Apparently you hadn't heard."

She flinched, and swallowed hard, and stared at me in a quick search for comfort I could not supply. She was a sturdy one, all right, a perfect size sixteen still getting along nicely with her second face lift and with her own hair, done in a classic Greek chignon discreetly henna-rinsed. Few people really deserve big money, but she might—her mind was quick and tough, her heart as warm as you could wish, although realistically under control. She was a nymph by choice instead of by compulsion, but she never pushed, or leaned, or made believe. "I liked him, Steve. I really did."

"He was a bit out of his depth. He didn't need that monocle. It may have tricked him visually when he crossed the street."

"When is the ceremony?"

"There won't be one here. I phoned this morning. He'll go back to Denmark on a plane tonight. The coffin will be closed."

"I see." She let her breath out, all the way. "We've both given up mourning long ago, dear, haven't we. But as it is, you won't approve of me and what I've got myself mixed up with now."

I sipped her vichyssoise and said: "Let's lay it on the line, please, Marcia. You're not bashful, and I'm in a hurry."

"It's those silly kids." She sounded half-embarrassed, half-defiant. "They're trying to hold me up."

"Are they? With what?"

"They're asking me to take them to New York."

"On *Miss Virginia*?" She nodded, eagerly. But she was holding out on me. "Why should you?"

"Steve, dear, need you ask?"

I shrugged and finished off the soup. She wasn't being coy. It merely seemed unnecessary to her rather than indelicate to go into details. She understood completely that I had no patience with her predilection for occasional young girls; she'd managed to confess to me, some years ago, that she felt foolish every time when it was over, but that while it lasted she just couldn't seem to get enough of it. There was no point in arguing with her about this one, not even if I'd had all afternoon. "Why don't you take the dolly on a little cruise and buy some airline tickets for her friends?"

"I thought of that. But it's not what they want."

The butler put a lobster salad plate before me, showed me a

half-bottle of a vintage Montrachet, and poured for my approval. It was five minutes to one, according to my watch, but the delay seemed unavoidable. When he had left again I said: "Come on now, Marcia, what's the snapper? Are they holding out for you to ship back that old Volkswagen or buy it from them?"

"No, it's gone. They traded it this morning. They got fifty kilograms of kif for it. That's what they'd like me to ship back."

I nearly choked on a big bite of lobster tail. Kif is Moroccan hashish, just about as potent as it comes, and fifty kilos of it should bring sixty thousand dollars or a little better, whole-sale, in New York. Try taking in a suitcase load or two through customs if you have that counterculture look.

A million-dollar private yacht is something else, such as the answer to the problem. "You're not telling me that you agreed?"

"No, dear, of course not."

"Get this right, please, Marcia. Don't allow that junk on *Miss Virginia*, no matter what you do. It happens to be legal in Morocco, more or less, but almost anywhere else in the world . . ."

"I know."

"But I'm not being helpful. Very well, I'll try to be. The course of true love shall not be constrained. Where are these people?"

"Valerie's upstairs." She didn't sound self-conscious about that, even a little bit. "The boys are in the pool. I told them I'd discuss this with you, and they didn't seem to mind."

"Get Mick McGowan up here. He's the chairman of the board. The others we don't need."

She rang the little silver bell that brought the butler's foot-man. It was 1:08. I should already have been on the dock waiting in line to get my passport reviewed page by page and watch ten dirty fingernails probing my luggage for forbidden currency. The kid with the Mongolian mustache came swaggering across the terrace in a black bikini jockstrap dripping water.

". . . Hey, man, what's doing?"

"Not too much," I said. "We have been talking here about this deal of yours. Sounds pretty good to me."

"Nothing in it for you, man," he said brazenly.

"Sure, that's all right. Glad to help out you fellows. Mrs. Ellis is a friend of mine, and she's had no experience with this stuff. I'll get it to New York for you, no charge."

Marcia sat watching me across the luncheon table; the bright hazel of her eyes was noticeably wider. The McGowan boy looked shocked. "You mean we turn it over to you, and you take it in, and you deliver it to us?"

"Did I say that?"

"Hey, right, you didn't. You just said you'd get it there." He bared an eyetooth for me. "Beautiful! Like you can rip off fifty keys of junk from us that way."

He didn't seem too worried about any other plans I might have for them. There was one I firmly had in mind. "What's wrong, man? Don't you trust me?"

"Shit, no. You're the enemy, you said last night."

"Oh, sure, but with connections. So you'll get a message from me in the morning how we put this thing together. Just forget about my ripping off you guys. You can hold the hash yourselves until you make the scene."

The funny thing was, he believed me. People usually do, if they're told forcefully enough what they would like to hear. But I had overplayed my hand with him, trying to beat the clock. "You're in the syndicate or something."

"Something. Run along, kid. Wait for your instructions. Follow them."

He nodded and slouched off. Marcia glanced after him uneasily. "You scared him, didn't you."

"Yes, I'm afraid so. Maybe that's exactly what he needs."

"What are you going to do to him?"

"Why, I'll fast-shuffle him into a Spanish jail, of course, what else? Him and those two other cool cats. The girl is your department." We were on our feet and making for the courtyard where the chauffeur Geoffrey had one of the Cads out with the motor running, and with my belongings on the back seat.

"Steve, dear, are you sure you wouldn't like me to call Captain Harvey?"

We embraced before I shook my head. There was no sense in advertising my arrival. *Miss Virginia* would have brought me the front page of the Marbella *Sun*. The car ferry to Málaga was scheduled to depart at three, and I could always take that and be something like five hours late.

"I'm sort of used to this."

"But Lita isn't." Marcia was honestly concerned, but she was not as well-informed as she believed herself. "You're really very naughty, both of you."

She'd been convinced of that almost two years now, which was not just preferable but imperative: she had no talent for discretion. Lita was extremely fond of her, and I had more than once been forced to stop them from exchanging confidences.

British chauffeurs in a hurry have more skill and guts than cab drivers in Tokyo. Geoffrey delivered me on smoking tires, six inches from the entrance to the dock shed at six minutes before two. The hydrofoil passenger agent, a young Arab in immaculate white nylon cords, snatched up my bags himself and dumped them inside on the nearest customs counter. "Sah, you very late." I shook his hand with a ten-dirham note. "We only hold your seat, sah, because Missus Ellis ask it on the telephone." The two Moroccan douaniers offered identical malicious scowls, waving away my export slip declaring foreign currency. "How many dirham, sah?" I gave them what they were entitled to expect, under the circumstances, and marched over to the window grille of the police booth, half-anticipating to run into Inspecteur Aziz. But there was only one more khaki uniform, one more black look cured by the banknote folded in my passport. When I stepped down on the cabin deck, the sleek white launch cast off its moorings and purred in reverse, leaving the jetty stairs. It swung around, made grumbling for the harbor mouth, passed through and heaved itself up on its skids as it snarled out into the Strait.

MARBELLA, SATURDAY, JULY 17.

The car that met me on the landing stage was a small Austin station wagon: room for two in front and for the groceries in back, a sewing machine motor and the customary humble-pie, inverted snob appeal. Jacinto Gómez drove it as if it might fall apart. He'd have looked better in a Patton tank, or in the general's Rolls Royce, a stocky, powerfully muscled Indio and a fine soldier, with that thirty-year patina on him of the honest pro, the senior noncom who only lives to carry out his orders. Such men make ideal servants, but they also make ideal death machines. I liked him very much, and I was very much afraid of him as well. We puttered through what used to be a little Spanish fishing village that had grown up in ten years into an international society resort while he assured me formally that the señora was *muy bien* and told me that she had decided *muy subito*, very suddenly, to visit Europe two weeks earlier than usual this summer. I said I was certainly delighted about that. He glanced at me as if I'd made a thoroughly unnecessary observation—any tradesman's pleasure with the prompt return of a good customer should be self-evident.

For a few miles of the new, four-lane coastal highway we rolled on in silence. At the Bahia Dorada turnoff he cut left across the overpass and carefully negotiated a driveway under the umbrella pines. Its narrow strip of asphalt terminated in the carport of the Villa Calayán.

A beach house on the Costa del Sol can mean almost anything, but this one wasn't kidding. It maintained a private, heated swimming pool right on the beach itself. Hybrid Bermuda grass provided the croquet lawn; cedars had been planted by the score, full grown, to overwhelm the pines. The private lodge presented a low profile of basalt rock and glass paneling, but it was trickily constructed on three levels, with the bottom floor exposing itself only landward, and assigned to servants' quarters and to storage space. A covered patio overlooked the sea and fronted the living room, two stories high and twenty meters long. The intricate interior brick and tile work had created something of a miniature cathedral aspect. I admired the craftsmanship involved, but I was used to it. I'd been a guest here on three previous occasions in the past two years.

Lita de Vargas occupied a free-form deck chair on the patio. Her smile for me was coolly regal when I came in view, mounting the shallow walkway from the lawn. She was a slender, darkly tanned brunette, still in her early thirties, with a quality of elegance—such women can wear daring gowns or, as on this occasion, an extreme bikini without stimulating lechery or disrespect. Her tea was being served by Ana Gómez, who was squat and coffee-brown, wore a housekeeper's black uniform, and who quite pointedly avoided seeing me until I spoke to her. "Ah! *Buenas tardes, Señor Harvester. Limón y azúcar para usted?*"

"*No, gracias, Doña Ana. Como siempre.*"

She displayed a scowl for this mild implication of reproach, although she knew, of course, that I don't use lemon or sugar. Lita waved her off, impatiently, and offered me four fingers to be kissed. "Hallo, my darling. You seem slightly *dégagé.* I've inconvenienced you, arriving two weeks early." Her Swiss finishing-school English came on accentless, deficient only in the

current idiom. I told her no, of course she hadn't inconvenienced me, and kissed her delicately scented wrist, and let
myself be urged into a chair and served a cup of tea. Ana
Gómez, Jacinto's wife, retreated to the kitchen, managing as
always to communicate her disapproval and, as usual, to set my
mind at rest.

"There are no difficulties?"

"None at all, my darling. Only those I've made for you
myself."

"And I for you."

She shook her head, arching her lovely neck. "No, never.
You're the most unselfish, the most understanding man, and
I'm a horrible, immodest, greedy woman. Hurry with your tea,
please, Steve."

"Will they expect us to . . ."

"Oh yes, they will. You know they will."

Her eyes were a cool shade of lilac green, but they held
mine with terrible intensity. I swallowed hard and contracted
my belly muscles to contain the fire that had begun to spread
within, and scrambled to my feet when she swung lithely off
her chair. We strolled into the house, through the vast living
room and under the Gauguin that dominated the east staircase
to the master suite. Its individually air-conditioned boudoir had
been done in Renaissance, including a Venetian sixteenth-cen-
tury four-poster with a beautifully if somewhat lubriciously
illustrated canopy and with a modern queen-size innerspring.
No doubt the decorator would have been ecstatic if he'd realized how relevant his concept of this room would prove itself.
It was a genuine coincidence, however, for the house had been
put up and decorated six or seven years ago.

The room had been our sanctuary, in a curiously frustrating,
ironic sense, for less than two.

I had met General Francisco Vargas Urticaria only once, in

Bogotá, and under circumstances of substantial embarrassment to both of us. These had originated on my side, one late November evening, with a phone call from New York. I caught a National Airlines flight from London to Miami that same night, and walked into Wayne Latimer's hospital room at breakfast time. He was a former FBI agent, in his late forties, sharper than a stainless steel tack but not in good physical condition. Gelusil and tranquilizers wouldn't always keep him going, and his temper would fall off accordingly. "Why you?" he greeted me. "You don't know South America. You've never even been there." When I told him everybody else was busy and that he'd deprived me of a holiday, he managed to control his sympathy. "You do speak Spanish?"

"Let's not worry about me so much," I said. "What's wrong with you?"

He said the medical profession had been trying to make up its mind if he should be cut open to find out. "They wanted to get on with it in Bogotá. I passed and grabbed a plane. Our customer is on the hospital board down there."

"He's a doctor?"

"So was Che Guevara."

Latimer looked pretty bad. I put a leash on my impatience and said pleasantly enough: "I know that, Wayne, but Jimmy Dexter mentioned that you were supposed to brief me. You can skip the generalities. Colombia has twenty million people. It's about the size of California and Texas put together. It's politically fairly stable, with a president elected for four years, a senate, and a house of representatives. Exports are coffee, oil, and emeralds. Havana has been trying for a long time but can't seem to get anything going there. Now tell me why."

"You see?" he scoffed, exasperated with me. "You don't have a clue. Take you three months to line this up, and you won't get three days." He had a spasm, bit it back, and bared his teeth at me. "Okay, I'll give it to you in one hunk. Castro *is* making progress. There's no reason why he should. The country's fairly prosperous. The Indios are a small minority, well-integrated. There's the usual agrarian-reform problem, and politics are elitist, of course. But you can't get away from those in South America. They need agrarian reforms in Cuba, in reverse, and *their* political elite is even more objectionable since it has no manners. In Colombia, they've organized a half dozen guerrilla outfits. Doesn't mean a thing, the army can take care of them. The only question is, who takes care of the army."

"Don't the politicians?"

"Sure they do, if you mean pay and rations. But there are too many first lieutenants crowding forty, and too many majors who'll never get a regiment."

The straw to make the bricks. Even in ancient Rome, if you were discontented with the government, you talked with four or five centurions and promised each of them a legion. "Who's your doctor friend?" I asked.

"Juan Ruiz-Martinez. Home and office in the Bolivar Hotel. A Castro-Maoist, but not responsible for the guerrilla picture. That's supposed to be controlled direct, by Cubans in the field. Ruiz-Martinez is a practicing Colombian physician. Almost all his patients are notorious radicals or student activists."

"His nurse sold you the list," I said.

"His janitor, for fifty pesos. Like three bucks. What should be worth a little more than that is which one of them will assassinate General Vargas. Also when and how."

"Who's he?"

"He's not the president," said Latimer, bitterly patient with me. "Or the chief of staff. He has been both, but he retired about ten years ago. To some extent he's the Colombian de Gaulle. You'll never meet him, and you wouldn't like him if you did."

"If he's all that important, they'll have tried before to take him out," I said.

"At least three times, but his protection's pretty good. This time they'll make it, our informant claims."

"The janitor?"

"No, no. The general's wife."

November is a rainy month in Bogotá, the Avianca hostess told me. My arrival late that afternoon, however, featured sunshine, a mild spring breeze, and the longest landing run I could remember suffering through. The city and its airport are at 8,700 feet.

The desk clerk at the Tequendama came up with a guest card to their country club.

I caught up on my sleep that night. At nine A.M. the golf pro found me waiting at his door. He had a fairly decent bag of clubs, a cart, and a small item of advice for me. "The party just ahead of you, señor. Do not disturb them, please." I said I wouldn't think of it, which was untrue, and parked near the first tee where, from a courteous distance, I watched Isabella Luz de Vargas hit a very creditable drive. She had a caddie but no partner, and no transportation. As she walked off down the fairway, two men in a pickup truck rolled from the service area along a trail that turned into the rough.

I did my warming up and waited until she'd moved almost out of sight, then fired an easy drive to follow her. The cart was a big help to me, of course. She was a walker, but I stayed behind at a respectful distance for six holes, closed in a little on the seventh, moved up on the eighth, and dropped a nice approach shot about ten yards short of where she was already lining up the green, her caddie at the flag. It made a more or less acceptable excuse for overtaking her on wheels.

"Good morning. I've replaced Wayne Latimer. My name is Stephen Harvester."

The pickup truck was coming fast; its driver plowed up quite a strip of turf when he slammed on his brakes. His partner had an automatic rifle on me. *"No se mueva, por favor, señor!"* I kept my hands in view, on the cart's steering wheel, and didn't move, as ordered. They were competent enough, but they'd forgotten that most laborers in overalls will shave, or trim their mustaches, only on weekends. When the driver started to jump out, Lita de Vargas stopped him with a hand wave. *"Esta bien, Jacinto. Señor Harvester es un amigo."*

She bestowed her queenly smile on me where he could see it. Both men stared at me, impassively, filing a mental picture of me; then the driver bowed to her and slipped behind the wheel again, and ruined some more turf going into reverse.

"I'm glad you managed to convince him," I said cheerfully.

"Why shouldn't he believe me? He has known me since I was a child."

She sounded cool and distant, and the smile had vanished. Latimer had warned me that I would dislike her, too, and he was right. I said: "Let's agree now on where we've met. Before Jacinto thinks of asking us."

"If he presumes to do that, I shall tell him you were at the same Columbus Day reception at your embassy, last month, where Mr. Latimer was introduced to me."

"No good."

"I beg your pardon?"

"He can check my passport. It'll show I was in England and in France last month."

". . . Very well, you were presented to me at a charity affair in August. In Monaco. By the Princess Grace herself. We danced."

I thought about that and said: "Better. Were you unescorted?"

"Always when I am in Europe, yes."

"All right, that'll be it. Finish your round and meet me for a cup of coffee on the clubhouse terrace, please."

She merely nodded, and I backed the cart away. She gave her ball a careless swipe that nearly missed the green and strode on after it.

Later, when she came to my table on the terrace, she looked very elegant indeed, as well as freshly showered, in a simple little cotton print that only an Italian couturier could have whipped up for her at, say, five hundred dollars. ". . . What has become of Mr. Latimer, please?"

"He has stomach trouble."

"Yes, of course." She put the matter from her mind. "Have you made progress?"

"I came in last night."

"Why did you wish to talk with me?"

I didn't. I detested her, and it was fairly obvious that she reciprocated. "Wayne suggested *you* might have made progress," I said coldly.

She released her breath in a long sigh. "But how? He knows the situation. He must have explained it to you. There is a young student of good family who has been socially acceptable to both my husband and myself, and who became—infatuated with me. It was he who blurted out to me in privacy, last week, that an attempt on us is being planned. If this succeeds, the army and the government are to be taken over by a group of radicals to which the boy himself belongs. He certainly would not have warned me if my life were not in danger, and he has refused to give me any further information."

"But he wants you to get out of Bogotá right now, and show your appreciation to him later. Is that it?"

Her eyes were green, and scornful of me. Latimer had told me all of this, and that she'd come to him with it because she'd sensed he was in a position to take action. She had made him promise that the boy would not be hurt, a promise she could never have extracted from her husband. Latimer, who knew about Dr. Ruiz-Martinez, had agreed to handle it. He had installed two spike mikes in the Bolivar Hotel that broadcast to a tape recorder in his office in the Esso Building, and he'd paid the janitor to keep a name-and-time log of all visitors. He had been getting interesting but not-yet-conclusive stuff until two days ago, when he'd thrown up a glass of milk that had turned red.

The answer might be waiting for me there. But it was clearly necessary first to come to terms with our informant. "Are you sure that this young man of yours . . ."

She cut me short, imperiously. "Quite sure, thank you. Or we should not be sitting here, discussing it. May I know what you plan to do?"

"Did Wayne explain his plans to you?"

He'd told me he had not. She said, too eagerly: "Of course he did." I shook my head and said I'd be in touch, got up and pulled her chair, and walked her to her car. Jacinto and his partner, who'd been loitering at the nearest corner of the clubhouse, were already in the front seat, wearing livery. The car was a Rolls Silver Cloud. I bowed over her hand, disliking her, and strolled away, aware of the green lilac eyes behind me, resting on my back.

Latimer's key opened a door describing him as the concesionario of an obscure brand of American refrigerators. His executive suite did not even bother with a secretarial desk. Its front room held two dusty display models and a box of literature several years old; the back room was much like my own on Oxford Street. I found the tape recorder, which was 15/16th, low fidelity, speech-activated, with a timer circuit. There were still a few feet on the current reel. I put a new one on, set up a separate playback deck, and went to work.

By eight o'clock that night I'd run through everything, including Latimer's old tapes and his interpretative notes.

That a conspiracy existed was beyond the slightest doubt. I

counted forty-six participants, in the available material. They were so fat and happy with their system of communication that it didn't seem to have occurred to them a doctor's office can be bugged as easily as any other place. Ruiz-Martinez sounded curiously indiscreet himself; he even made me wonder if he might be a police provocateur, and if perhaps another tape recorder might be picking up these fascinating conversations at the jefatura, seven blocks away. It certainly would be of interest there to find out the name of the new chief, and of his boss, the minister of the interior, and *his* boss, the new president. The army, too, might like to hear about who would be in command of it, and of its more important units. All of this as of November twenty-third. The day after tomorrow.

There were various discussions of the ways and means to bring these things about, of course. Company X would occupy the television station, squadrons Y and Z the presidential palace. Regiments in Barranquilla, Medellín, and Cali were to deal with this and that. Soldiers will follow orders, even if they don't completely understand why certain officers have suddenly replaced their seniors. Unless a voice speaks up, a voice of great authority, commanding very much respect.

The name of General Francisco Vargas was not mentioned on the tapes. Almost inevitably, the conspirators had started by deciding how he'd be disposed of, and by whom. Wayne Latimer must have plugged into them too late, probably much too late—perhaps a month or more. At this stage there was little need for any more discussion of the matter. All I could dig up was a few cryptic references that might very easily apply to some entirely different and minor aspect of the plot. *We can depend on Major Robles* (nothing in the context specified for what), and, *If Ortega does his job* . . . (Unspecified again. The speaker was the future minister of justice. His remark was interrupted by a mutter of consensus.) There were many more, but I liked these two best. One reason was that neither of these names appeared on the good doctor's list of patients. Or on the log of visitors kept by the janitor.

I locked up the material, and for a while stood by the only window, looking out. I had missed lunch and hardly noticed it. The city, glistening under the night rain of late spring, loomed even larger than I had anticipated. Bogotá has more than two million people, and the notion that so many could be taken over by so few seemed utterly absurd. Yet it was feasible, I knew that very well. It might even prove easy. Just two bullets might turn out to do the trick, and one of these would very nicely keep Señora Isabella Luz de Vargas from perhaps reaching a radio station, or a barracks, or some other place where she'd be talking out of turn. Too many wives of surplus generals have caused too many problems all through history.

Tomorrow night would be the night, I thought, and wondered about Julio Guzmán.

He was the one who'd urged her to leave town. I had him on the tape, several times; he sounded very young, and terribly sincere. Apparently he led a delegation of the student activists involved. Jacinto and his partner would have needed about twenty minutes, wringing him out dry.

But there were other methods. This must have occurred to Latimer as well, because he'd made a casual surveillance of the boy. I checked his notes, went back to my hotel room, changed to a dark suit but did not shave. A steak and salad at La Pampa served to fuel me. It was still early for Colombia, around eleven, when my taxi found what I was looking for, the little coffee bar, one of a dozen in the district bordering the university.

He wasn't difficult to spot, although the others at his table were much like him: early twenties, medium-long hair, cheap slacks, expensive sweaters. But they were deferring to him, not unreasonably—the charisma of the budding politician draped him like a flag and strongly underscored his dark good looks.

The group was eating *empañadas*, pancakes filled with spiced ground meat, and still the volume of their conversation shook the walls. I leaned my back against the bar, had coffee, and deliberately put the evil eye right on the kid. It took a little while. He wasn't stupid or insensitive, but he was busy. When he did become aware of me he stiffened visibly. I jerked my chin in the direction of the back door and walked out that way. The alley was a mud bath hissing with the rain, but there were garbage cans in a small service court under a strip of roof. The ambiance was exactly right.

I'd never been in South America before, as Latimer had pointed out, but I knew Mexico, and knew it well enough to pass, under the circumstances, for a certain type of Mexican. When Julio Guzmán appeared he found me sitting on a crate, legs crossed, the collar of my trench coat up over my ears. "They told me you were faster on your feet than this, señor," I said.

The phrase, in Mexican, sounds fairly crude. He closed the door, reluctantly. *"Qué quiere?"*

"Major Robles sent for me."

We can depend on Major Robles. Therefore, if he sent for somebody like me, he had his reasons. Julio Guzmán accepted that, of course. "I see. But to what purpose?"

"It is now considered necessary to provide a jockstrap for tomorrow night, señor," I said, and spat into the alley past his feet.

He understood me very well. What I was telling him was that there had been a decision to employ a Mexican professional to back up the assassin. It was dark, but I could almost taste and smell his consternation. ". . . At Casa Rosaleda?" I ignored that, struck a match, and lit a cigarette, allowing him to see my sneer. "But what . . . Why do you come to me with this?"

"You are familiar with the house, señor. You have a car."

That was more like it. He could breathe again, almost too audibly. *"Muy bien.* Where shall I meet you? At what time?"

"The bottom station of the cable car, señor. You name the time. It is your city, and your car."

"I shall be there at three o'clock tomorrow night."

It was pathetically obvious what he had in mind. I grunted at him, tramped off through the alley, reached the street, and found my taxi where I'd left it down the block. By then I'd pretty well decided how to put a handle on the situation. Latimer had given me the number of her private phone. I rang it with the sun over my early breakfast table. "You'll be at the club this morning?"

"Yes, as usual."

"I wanted to make sure. I'll join you if I may."

"Of course, with pleasure, Mr. Harvester," she told me distantly. "Thank you for asking me. Goodbye." The phone clicked in my ear and offered me a dial tone. I caught myself just short of slamming it. No woman had come close to irritating me as much as this in many years. I passed up what was left of breakfast, underdressed deliberately, then concluded that Bermuda shorts might give her the idea that I was trying to look younger than my age.

She was ten minutes late, which almost brought me into conflict with the female foursome booked for a 9:30 start. When she arrived, a fashion plate straight out of *Vogue*, they knew her, fawned on her, and held us up some more while I was being introduced and scrutinized. Then she banged out a two hundred-yard drive, not even troubling to warm up, and I produced a slice that screamed about three hundred, right over the clubhouse roof. Nobody laughed, not even when my second ball popped up.

We walked to it along the fairway, in dead silence, and she stood by hipshot like a model, watching me compose myself and fire my normal brassie distance, halfway to the green. She made no comment as we strolled behind our caddies. I said: "Is your house named Casa Rosaleda?"

"Yes, it is. Didn't you know?"

"My dear lady, I just got here, and Wayne's records don't happen to mention it. The name came up last night and seemed to fit. I have exciting news for you. Your husband's murder has been scheduled for tomorrow morning early, probably at two A.M. You were supposed to be included. But when you pretended to ignore your Mr. Guzmán's warning, he apparently decided to work out something for you. My guess would be that he has made a private deal with the assassin. I imagine that between them they'll just lock you up somewhere for a few days. Until their revolution's running in the groove."

She didn't even glance at me. We'd found her ball, and she reached for a three-wood, hacked away, and landed smartly on the green, about six inches from the cup. We walked, and she asked coolly: "Are you certain?"

"No. There's no such thing. I want to check out two more names with you. Ortega?"

". . . I've met Señora Carmen Torres de Ortega. She's a widow in her eighties, socially important. And I know two tradesmen by that name."

"We've missed on that score. Major Robles?"

"Which one? There must be as many as a dozen in the army. Surely you're aware that Spanish surnames cannot be identified that way. You need the first name and the mother's name as well, and even then . . ."

"Do you know any Major Robles?"

"Personally? No. There is one in the Ministry of War. He's the assistant bureau chief of personnel assignment, I believe."

That was more like it, but I made no comment. My ball had an easy lay, and I got on the green with it right next to hers. She was two up on me, but not for long. I shot the nine in 37, beating her by three, enjoying it. Along the service road,

Jacinto's pickup truck kept pace, although I never caught him or his partner watching us.

As we approached the locker rooms she asked me quietly: "May I know what you propose to do?"

"Arrange for an abortion."

". . . I beg your pardon?"

"My dear lady, you don't *want* a revolution in this country, do you? Even a suppressed one? Neither do my people, so let's just not have one."

"Can you stop it?"

"Yes, I think so. Maybe even without inconveniencing your husband."

"I'd appreciate that very much," she carefully assured me. "But I don't quite understand."

I smiled at her, disliking her. There really wasn't much to smile about. I wasn't going to perform card tricks or do anything particularly clever. Latimer had done his job and made it easy for me. "Just in case," I said, "what are your husband's plans tonight? And yours?"

"We expect friends for bridge and a light supper. They'll have left by two." Routine security was fairly good, as she explained when I asked about it. The estate was walled, and wired against intruders. Visitors and tradesmen at the gate faced a closed-circuit television camera. She had no children, and at night only Jacinto and an adjutant stayed in the house itself; the servants' quarters were some fifty yards away.

I told her that if there were any problems I'd get back in touch, bowed to her, and left her there. With any luck at all I'd make the early morning Pan Am flight back to Miami. I was certainly not interested in her understanding, or her appreciation, or in ever seeing her again. I caught a taxi back to the hotel and changed, walked to the Esso Building, spent about two hours checking out the current tape, and found what I'd expected—nothing much. There had been no more conferences because none were needed. They were set to go.

Dr. Juan Ruiz-Martinez had been seeing a few real patients. He appeared to specialize in what are tactfully defined as male disorders. I got through to him by phone when he returned from lunch, declared myself a tourist at the Tequendama, and in my best broken Spanish started to explain that I'd been with a woman a few days ago, and now there was something I'd like to talk to him about. He interrupted me in passably good English. "Who referred you to me, sir?"

I said that I was very happy he could speak my language. Didn't he know that his name was listed in a confidential travel guide for members of the Lions Club? It seemed he didn't and that he was much amused by it. He gave me an appointment at five-thirty. For a while I listened to the tape recorder monitor, but he made no suspicious phone calls; he just rang the desk at the hotel to ask if I was registered. By five o'clock I'd finished at the Esso Building, packaged the material, and typed a résumé of it. Then I called Latimer's crunch contact at the embassy and told him where to find it if he didn't hear from me again by seven on the dot.

Political conspiracies, except some of the wild-eyed Middle-East variety, always provide themselves with a fail-safe routine. These can be simple, and they usually work out pretty well, when somebody discovers the red light on the control board. Juan Ruiz-Martinez saw it right away. He had admitted me himself into his empty waiting room, and looked me over, and had been unable to conceal his agitation. I was rather obviously not a member of the Lions Club.

"Excuse me, please. I have another patient."

He retired into his office, tried to close the door, and found me on his heels. He was a bantam weight in a white jacket, pale and intellectual, with the obligatory little black mustache, but in my thirty years of pottering around the edges I'd come up against a few more like him. It was very necessary to bring up a knee under his spine. He bounced off his examination table, tripped over the chair I kicked into his way, and scuttled for his desk. By then I was behind it with the drawer open and his deadly little German Mauser pistol in my pocket.

". . . Take it easy doctor. There's no hurry."

"Who are you, sir?"

"You've got my name right here in your appointment book. It's as I told you on the phone, doctor, we have something to talk about." He had recovered his composure. He picked up the toppled chair and used it, gingerly; his stare at me where I was sitting on his desk relayed the obvious message of distrust and disaffection. "Money," I said cheerfully. "A lot of money. Such as twenty thousand pesos every three months. We'll call it a retainer for professional services."

The peso in Colombia is worth about six cents, but he was not a wealthy doctor. He was interested, and confused, and trying to pretend. "Even a life insurance company pays more than that," he slowly pointed out.

"Not ours, doctor. We throw in free life insurance. You're going to need some, by tonight."

That got us down to basics. "What is it you wish to buy?"

"You, doctor. It's that simple."

There's an elementary technique in counterespionage, known as the turnaround. It wouldn't have worked out with Che Guevara, but this man looked right for it, which was why Latimer had gone for him even before Señora Isabella Luz de Vargas showed up on the screen. Dr. Ruiz-Martinez knew exactly what I had in mind, by then. He didn't have to like it, but it was a reasonable proposition. I was offering protection and a fee, of sorts, if he'd agree to work for us.

A double agent has his problems staying healthy. Still, it must have seemed to him he didn't have much choice. He said: "You take a lot for granted, Mr. Harvester."

"You don't believe that, doctor."

"Are you telling me that you are of the CIA, and the police have been informed about tomorrow's—schedule of events?"

"Oh, that," I said. "We've known about that for six weeks. You're going to turn that off, of course. The warning code is *calderón*."

It shouldn't have surprised him, but he winced and cursed me anyway. His English ripened into weary pathos. ". . . Have you no eyes, no shame? My country suffers. It needs surgery."

"I wouldn't know, doctor. It doesn't need Fidel or Mao. Or a bunch of discontented officers and politicians who haven't made the grade. Shall we get on the phone and save the firing squad a lot of work?"

He asked me slyly whom I wanted him to call. When I produced the list he glanced at it and shuddered. Then he pulled the phone across the desk. I told him not to get involved in explanations, warned him that my Spanish was as good as his, and prodded him along. But it takes time to complete forty-six connections, many of them on long distance, even if you're only trying to identify your party and communicate a single pregnant word to him. You get a lot of busy signals and wrong numbers, and a lot of wives who can't be sure just when their husbands will be home. We were still at it by eleven, long after I'd called the embassy myself and taken Latimer's man off the hook.

Then it occurred to me, belatedly, that there were two more names. They were, of course, the first two I should have attended to. But all of us are capable of folly, or stupidity, or mental block, as the case may be. "Catch Robles and Ortega while you're at it, doctor, will you please?"

He stared at me, a complicated stare, part stricken, part defiant. He, too, had forgotten, so to speak. He dialed rapidly and listened to the ringing signal, disconnected, tried again, and shook his head. "It is too late."

"What do you mean, too late? Where are they?"

"I don't know, sir. Major Robles carries the responsibility for the elimination of General Vargas *y su señora*. Captain Rafael Ortega is to execute it and report to me. But none of us were made acquainted with their plans."

We can depend on Major Robles. "Wrong," I said. "Call Julio Guzmán. He knows." The student activists had been the last ones on my list because they were the least important. My reluctant helper was already dialing and listening, biting his lips. I noticed with considerable irritation that I was perspiring, which was most unusual for me without exercise.

"There is no answer. I am sorry."

"Call the Bar Café Mercedes," I said harshly, throwing him the phone book. He complied, got through, was told that Julio Guzmán had not come in. I took the phone away from him and rang the private number of her ladyship at Casa Rosaleda, let it ring twice, changed my mind, and banged down the receiver. "There's still time. I'll go myself. Complete the list, please, doctor. Then you'll have to get out of the country like the others, until this blows over. Tell 'em you discovered that your office had been bugged, which happens to be true. Report to me by mail at postbox 400, London West One."

He had that enigmatic stare for me again. "What if my memory should fail me, sir?"

"I'd move to Cuba or to China in that case, if I were you."

He nodded, sadly, as if he could see my point, and started dialing. I walked out of his office, sprinted down two flights of stairs into the lobby of the Bolivar Hotel, and lost ten minutes like so many hours hunting for a taxi in the rain. It was already close to midnight when the driver pulled up at the gate and eyed me in his rear-view mirror. "Here it will be necessary for you to descend, señor, and push the button."

This was set in a white metal box under a spotlight mounted on the gate itself. Both wall and gate looked duly formidable; it would take heavy equipment to contend with them. I got out in the rain and pushed the button, activating a whole bank of floodlights and a slide in the white box that bared the lens of the closed-circuit camera. A grille-protected speaker cleared its throat and asked my name. When I supplied it there was a brief silence, then: "*Lo siento mucho, señor*, you are not expected."

That would be the adjutant on duty. "This is urgent business, and highly confidential," I said. "Please check with Doña Isabella. She will authorize you to admit me."

"She is entertaining guests, señor, and cannot be disturbed. You will be good enough to telephone for an appointment in the morning."

With a click the bank of floods dimmed out. I turned back to my driver, paid him off, and sent him on his way. A witness to my further conversation with the adjutant I didn't need.

The situation was a little delicate. A German or a Frenchman, even an Italian, would have listened to me with the possibility in mind of changing his decision. But the Spanish temperament, admirable otherwise, doesn't accommodate itself to flexibility. The adjutant would be inclined not to believe a word I said.

I was still wasting an allotted sixty seconds' mental concentration on the problem when a silver blue Ferrari growled out of the traffic on the avenue and screamed down to a stop beside me with its headlights glaring at the gate. The driver did not even see me. He burst from the car, stabbed at the button, stood under the lights, and showed himself as Julio Guzmán wearing a dinner jacket, getting wet. But he was recognized: the floods clicked off, the electronic gate hummed open. He flung himself back behind the wheel, and had the car in gear and rolling before he became aware of me sitting beside him with the little Mauser pistol in my lap.

He hit his brakes so hard he would have pitched me through the windshield if I hadn't braced myself for that con-

tingency. He even tried to take the gun away from me. I had
to force him back against the headrest with a forearm crushing
in his Adam's apple. *"Un momento, niño!* I have news for
you." But he continued clawing at me, gasping for breath until
the code got through to him. "It's *calderón*, Guzmán! You understand me? *Calderón!* Where is Captain Ortega? We must
stop him!"

". . . You are not Mexican." He actually sounded like a child.
"Where is Ortega?"

I'd released him, and he slumped over the wheel, groaning,
debilitated by frustration and bewilderment. "He . . . is here.
He will not . . . act until I join him. Who has authorized the
cancellation code?"

"Ruiz-Martinez, niño. Let us find Ortega."

Shakily, he managed to restart his engine and to put the big
Ferrari back in gear. The driveway wandered through severely
landscaped grounds, then passed the formal rose bower that
gave the place its name. Only two other vehicles were in the
parking plaza, one of them a Daimler limousine, the other a
plain khaki Ford with military markings. Lights blazed on the
ground floor through eight huge French windows curtained in
damask. The double row of coach lamps on the porch steps
lent an almost festive air. I'd slipped the Mauser back into the
pocket of my dripping raincoat, following the kid up to the
massive wrought-iron and plate glass front door, which he
opened with an easy familiarity, leaning his weight on it. A
vestibule paved in Carrara marble, decorated with Italian an-
tiques, confronted us. The anteroom immediately to our left
must have been large, but it looked inconsiderable by comparison. It had been furnished with austerity and in a regimental
manner with crossed swords and standards on the walls, and
battle paintings, and with a big table covered in green baize
that bore a television monitor and a control panel. Behind this,
from a swivel chair, rose a tall man in his late thirties who

wore ceremonial uniform flashing with silver fourragères.

His rank insignia were unfamiliar to me, and there was no time to study them. He recognized me from the monitor, of course; I had anticipated that, and I was ready with my little speech. But it was not the right one. I was tired, and slow, and I had failed to grasp the obvious. Major Robles, she had told me, was a war ministry officer in charge of personnel assignment. He could place disgruntled juniors, by the score, in staff positions with the power tap conveniently near at hand. He also could replace the trusted ADC to an ex-president, for one night, on some plausible excuse, and keep himself out of the way.

Captain Rafael Ortega took one look at me and at the cheerless and bedraggled youth accompanying me. His reflexes were too fast for his own good; I found out later that he was on the Olympic team, both as a horseman and a fencer. He attempted the impossible, which was to get his hands on the machine pistol racked up under the table out of sight and cover me with it before my own reflexes pulled the trigger in my pocket. "*Calderón*, you idiot," I said, about a second and a half too late. The insult was intended to apply to both of us.

He stared at me in utter disbelief, and at his own right arm in which my bullet had smashed through the artery and probably through half the motor nerves. He looked like a good man, accustomed to the best in life, and certainly accustomed to his body functioning efficiently, responsive to his bidding. I felt sorry as all hell for him, and for myself. There wasn't one damn thing that I could do for him, at this point. If he kept his mouth shut I could save the boy, but that was all.

"Put on a tourniquet," I said.

The kid yanked out a handkerchief, snatched up a ruler from the table. He'd been briefly paralyzed, then jolted into action. Evidently he'd had training in first aid; he got Ortega's pulsing spout of blood under control immediately. His patient leaned against the wall, below the crossed Colombian and presidential flags, and watched him at his work. By then both of them were expressionless, almost detached.

Behind me, in the doorway to the vestibule, someone demanded irritably: "What has happened here, señores?"

I swung round, keeping both hands in view. This proved to be a sound idea, because Jacinto had another machine pistol on me with the trigger slack already taken up, his finger knuckles gleaming white. The man beside him actually looked a little like de Gaulle. But the resemblance was just facial—he was not particularly tall, and rather stocky. He wore dinner clothes as if he lived in them. His tan had that distinctive healthy glow; he might be seventy, but he was evidently durable.

Behind him in the vestibule Señora Isabella Luz de Vargas, pale as milk, stood with her guests. They were, as far as I could make out at a glance, just two more people: elderly, aristocratic, troubled but composed. "It would be pleasant to assure Your Excellency that this was an accident," I said.

"No doubt it would, señor. For you." He wasn't the least little bit amused with me. I was a dangerous intruder who'd shot up one of his officers, in gangster style, my coat stinking of scorched wet gabardine. The only thing that had to puzzle him would be the presence of the kid. "What is the purpose of your visit, Julio?" he carelessly inquired.

I said: "Señor Guzmán was kind enough to drive me here, and to secure admission for me at the gate."

That didn't bowl him over, but it sounded true if inexplicable. It meant that there was something more to this. Jacinto's trigger finger had relaxed, I noticed, and his eyes came slightly out of focus in a sidelong glance at his employer's wife. She noticed it, but she was forced to speak up anyway, of course. "This is the gentleman I've mentioned meeting at the club, Francisco," she said formally. "His name, you may recall, is Stephen Harvester. General Vargas, Señor and Señora Escobar."

Her guests murmured polite acknowledgments. Her husband's stare at me changed character, although not necessarily increasing its benevolence, so far as I could tell. "Why did you shoot?" he asked me bluntly.

"General, if I had not, both you and Doña Isabella would have died. Most probably within ten seconds."

"Please explain."

"Captain Ortega has a private grievance," I said carefully. "He planned to have himself assigned here for one night. This afternoon he boasted to a woman of these plans. She happens to be one of our informants."

Silence clogged the room. None of us moved an inch except the boy, and he only to readjust the tourniquet. At last, Vargas inquired: "You are of the United States intelligence, señor?" I just stared back at him, not answering him. "Can you prove this accusation?"

"Yes, Your Excellency. If I have to."

Vargas took his eyes off me, glanced at the automatic weapon on the floor. "Captain Ortega?"

The big man in blood-stained ceremonials said coldly: "He is right, the Yanqui."

Vargas sighed and held his hand out to me. "Let me have your gun, please, Señor Harvester," he said. He took the little Mauser I'd removed from Dr. Juan Ruiz-Martinez's desk drawer and gave it to Jacinto. Then he nodded at the self-confessed assassin. "Take him out," he ordered wearily.

At the hotel I walked my room for a long time. It was a good-sized room; it gave me eighteen paces straight across. There was a bottle of Black Label on the dresser, with a siphon and an ice bucket from Room Service to keep it company. As we all know, whisky is a depressant and should be avoided under stress, but somehow you don't think of that. You think of other things, such as the distant crack of a small pistol, and the whimper of distress beside you from the long-haired man-child fumbling with his starter key and suddenly collapsing on the wheel. No, Julio, there is no Santa Claus. The Rafael Ortegas of this world are not allowed to try again. They commit suicide.

If you must be a revolutionary, copy Major Robles. Then you won't need anyone like me to save your skin for you.

That had got through to him. He'd covered the ten miles or so back to the Tequendama with me in about six minutes. The Ferrari 365GT goes supersonic on you, if you let it. In Colombia, it'll cost your parents about sixty thousand dollars, duty paid.

The phone started to ring when I unlocked my door. " . . . I must speak with you."

"Sorry. My plane's at nine A.M."

"I mean right now. I'm coming over."

"Have you lost your mind?"

"Expect me, please." She had hung up on me again.

It turned out that her version of right now was something like an hour and a half. I walked my eighteen paces, wearing furrows in the rug, and used up half a bottle of depressant without notable effect. When she came in without so much as bothering to knock I happened to be in the bathroom. She could see and hear me, but she made no comment or excuse; she fixed herself a drink and sat down on the bed with it. She'd changed from dinner dress into gray jersey slacks with matching tunic and rebozo. Her umbrella dangled from a chair back, dripping on my furrowed wall-to-wall.

I watched her from the bathroom doorway for a while. At last I said: "Three guesses. One, he was your lover, and you're here to settle my account."

"Have you been drinking?"

"Yes, of course. Two, you've grown tired of living. Since we hate each other, it occurred to you to take me with you where you're going. Three, you do this all the time. Your husband doesn't care."

She glanced at me over her shoulder. "Do you have a cigarette? I came away without my purse." I found her one and struck a match for her. She took it from my slightly shaky fingers, used it, blew it out, and tossed it in a corner. ". . . My husband knows I'm here. He often has suggested this. He has been impotent for many years."

"He has suggested it? You mean like whisky, for medicinal purposes?"

"That is his thought."

I made a sound that may have been identifiable as laughter. "Considerate of him. Has it been beneficial to you, this medicine?"

"Do you believe I should have taken it?"

By then I had my back to her, making myself another drink. I needed to do something with my hands to keep from hitting her. "Well, haven't you?"

"Of course not."

In the dresser mirror she looked ice-cream cool. "About a week ago," I said, "you heard from Julio Guzmán about this little fracas that was in the works. You came to us instead of to your husband. You demanded our protection of the boy."

"I had more confidence in you than in our own security organization. I was right."

"You told Wayne Latimer a different story."

"Did I?"

"Oh, come on. The kid has no experience, but he's a radical, no question about that. Why should you worry over him? They would've packed him off to jail for a few months, or put him in a sanatorium. His family . . ."

"My husband would have had him killed."

"Why?"

"He'd have been convinced, as you are, that there was something between us. That would have been unacceptable to him. Please, let me show you." She extended her left hand; I turned back from the mirror to inspect it. It was small, and beautifully kept, but there were four small scars a fraction of an inch apart, about an inch above the wrist. "Three years ago a young French diplomat paid me a great deal of attention. I was—interested, but of course I knew that nothing could be done about it. I did not encourage him. But he was stubborn, and perhaps a little obvious, and when my husband spoke to him one evening at a small dinner party there was trouble. I'd had one glass of champagne too many and tried foolishly to intervene. I wound up with a fork driven into my hand, as a reminder of whose property I was. *He* had a hunting accident. Within two weeks."

"Fatal?"

"Oh yes. What you don't understand is that I'm not supposed to get *involved*."

She rose and put her empty glass down on the dresser, facing me. I said contemptuously: "And you've never taken medicine before."

"No, and I never shall."

Green lilac eyes reached up to mine, grew wider, deeper, drawing me into them, drowning me. I came up shuddering for air and realized that we'd been kissing for a long time, clinging to each other, mouths locked hard together and already thoroughly explored, but drinking from each other thirstily. Emotional inversion can be gradual, but when it is explosive it'll blow your mind. I was so much in love with her and wanted her so badly, I felt stupid, clumsy, nauseated, ill, and she herself seemed not much better off. She choked for breath, tearing herself away from me. "*Tell me you love me! Please!*"

"I love you. I don't know what's happened to us, but I . . ."

"Say I love you, Lita. Call me by my name."

"Lita. I love you, Lita."

"Prove it to me! Take me!" She was trying to undress, and

sobbing with frustration at a faulty zipper. When it broke she ripped it out and burst out into laughter, kicking off her slacks. "I can't go back like this. You're stuck with me!"

I slapped her, spinning her around. She fell across the bed, abandoning herself to me, still wearing her bikini panties. I stood over her, biting my tongue in vain—the words forced themselves through somehow. "You *didn't* sleep with Julio Guzmán?"

"No! Please *believe* in me!"

We were so good together it was frightening. She gave me back my youth, and I released in her the tensions that had built up through twelve years of unsuccessful marriage. But there was more, of course: a genuine ardor for each other that exceeded greatly the emotional involvement she had undertaken to deny herself. "Doesn't your husband realize . . . ?"

"No, no, my darling. Can't you see you're perfect, from his point of view? A Yanqui working for a living. Obviously you are unaccomplished and uncultured, and you have no money."

"Sure I do. I'm worth over a hundred thousand dollars. I've got tax problems."

"Please don't be silly. You're in the same category as Colombian peasants and Italian gigolos. I've been encouraged to experiment with both, at one time and another. Which reminds me, I'm supposed to pay you."

"Beautiful! How much?"

"Whatever we negotiate . . . no, not like that. I'm serious, you'll have to take a check and cash it, you can give the money to a home for wayward girls or something but it's terribly important that Francisco never suspects—*ohmydarling look at you!* Be careful, please. You'll hurt me."

"Tell me more about the money. I'm enjoying that."

"All right. I'll write you a big check for lots of money. Not my own money, my husband's money—*aaah!* That's what you wanted me to say, you ghastly pervert. So that you could

punish me, like this, and hurt me hurt me hurt me—hurt me
—love me—love me—*lovemeee* . . .!"
"No. You're getting off too easily . . . You'll have to
suffer—longer—more—before I'll let you—let you . . ."
"You can't stop me. You can't stop yourself. You can't you
can't you can't you *now*! Nownownownownownow! Oh marvelous. Oh utterly supremely marvelous. Tell me again now!
Say my name!"

I said her name; she had not yet called me by mine. She left
at five A.M., with her rebozo as a belt to hide the broken zipper. From my window I could watch the general's Silver Cloud
drive off with her along Carrera Diez.

Her thousand-dollar check I cashed that afternoon, at the
Miami branch of the Chase National, and put my own check in
the mail to the Red Cross. I visited Wayne Latimer, who
wasn't very interested; they had done a good deal more repair
work on him than he had been looking for. Then I reported to
New York by phone and reconfirmed my two weeks' leave.

She called me at the Fontainebleau that evening, as arranged. The next day I flew to Jamaica, found a cottage at the
Tower Isle, and met her plane at four. She'd carried off her
end of it. Permission for a further course of treatment had
been granted. But she'd been assigned a retinue: Jacinto
Gómez and his wife. For her protection and for our convenience.

It meant we had to set a constant watch over ourselves.
There is a quite considerable difference between the public
conversation and behavior of lovers and those of a lady with
her chartered fancy man.

The Spanish beach house was acquired that winter, to be
placed at our disposal for two weeks in February and in August. Somehow we'd come through almost two years of taking
part in this degrading farce.

Wayne Latimer recovered and was transferred to Manila.

Dr. Juan Ruiz-Martinez disappeared from sight. No mail from him came to my London postbox. I was not especially surprised. You play the averages in this game.

DEFENESTRATION

MARBELLA, SUNDAY, JULY 18.

Breakfast was served beside the pool. I was already slightly winded from my twenty laps of it, at top frustration speed. Lita was drifting on a plastic mattress, eating orange slices, and ignoring me.

I had four problems, three of them inconsequential.

One of these was the Rumanian affair, because it would require me to return to Tangier, probably within the week, for several days. Another was Leon de Bas and his preposterous demand for hostages I'd promised to "consider." Least of all, there was the Strawberries' attempt to hold up Marcia Ellis. That one I intended to dispose of with two phone calls, one of them to the assistant chief of Spanish customs at the airport, thirty miles away in Málaga.

The fourth problem could be more suitably described as a dilemma, since it posed two equally unbearable alternatives.

It usually pays, in circumstances such as these, to clear the deck. I drained my coffee cup and said I would be back in a few minutes. "Want to take a walk along the beach?"

"Of course, darling." She sounded listlessly composed.

I walked into the house and found a phone. I didn't worry about being overheard. The Gómez couple knew I was in business that had no bearing upon theirs with me. The Spanish lines are monitored, like everybody else's, but I wasn't planning any serious indiscretions. Don Antonio Molina worked on Sundays, in the heavy tourist months. He was one of the new breed, born after the civil war, the bright young men unscarred by ancient truculence or sorrow and intent only on personal ambitions and their family's prosperity. *"Esteban 'Arvester! Qué tal, amigo? Qué te pasa?"*

"Nothing much, Antonio," I said. "We have two possibilities to contemplate. First, there's a chance that on tonight's plane from Tangier a slight irregularity will be committed."

"Ah, sí, cómo no? On every airplane from Morocco we expect irregularities, during the season. Most of them are children, from your country and from England, Scandinavia, Holland, Germany. They wear much hair, also blue cotton pants, and dirty faces. They have very little money. If they carry drugs, we put them into prison for five years. We have more than a hundred of them now."

"Maybe you'll catch three more tonight," I said. "Another thing, Antonio. Suppose I had a tourist friend in Spain who didn't want to see the sights. Of course he should, so I'd be thinking about hiring somebody to escort him, wouldn't I. Anyone you'd care to recommend?"

He laughed at me, not very hard. "A persuasive escort, Esteban?"

"Oh, certainly. *Con mucho persuasión.*"

He asked me for my phone number. I gave it to him, promised him we'd get together soon, and flashed the operator back. In Tangier, Marcia's English butler told me that she wasn't yet available, but he dragged one of the three boys out of the pool for me. It was the black one, Hero Pud. "Hey, man, what's happening?"

"Where's Mick?"

"Not here, man. He's like interested in that crazy chick at the El Djinn. I'll pass the word to him."

"You'd better write this down," I said. "Iberia Flight 392, tonight. Leaves Tangier 20:20 hours, arrives Málaga 21:55. It's only half an hour, but there's an hour's difference in local time. I've just confirmed the reservations for you guys, you can pick up three tickets at the airline office, 35 Boulevard Pasteur. Buy two new suitcases, pack the merchandise in those, and take them with you on the plane."

"How'll we get through customs, man?" he cheerfully inquired.

"No problem in Morocco. Just don't try to take out any dirham currency, that's all. In Spain somebody'll meet you at the airport and take care of you."

He sounded happy but he wanted to know everything. Málaga was groovy, but the bread was in New York. I had to do my Bugsy Siegel bit again, the big shot from Las Vegas who does favors for his jet-set pals; you ask him how, he'll cut your kidneys out. The boy tried sniggering at me and didn't bring it off. He promised to round up the others and to hustle with the plane tickets. He didn't even mention Val. Apparently the three of them were satisfied that she was in good hands.

The phone rang almost on the instant I hung up. A heavy male voice with an Andalusian accent asked my name. "You wish to hire a guide, señor?"

"Two guides, I think. My friend is big, and he can be unreasonable."

"*Está bien.* We are not inexperienced in such matters. When do you require this service?"

"Probably tomorrow night."

The caller grunted and proposed a meeting. Did I have a car? What make and model? *Bueno*, I should park in it at Kilometro One Hundred and Eighty of the Carretera de Cadiz, at nine o'clock that night.

Lita had finished breakfast and had slipped into a white lace cover-up chemise. We started down the beach without a word.

The walk was one we'd taken scores of times before, though never in this mood. There wasn't much more than a mile of it, the first half shaded by the pines. The second, the return leg down the water's edge, took in a little cove under an outcropping of granite rock. This offered adequate seclusion and some fairly clean white sand, but not a great deal more. The blue Mediterranean still looks inviting, from a distance; closer by, its blotchy iridescence will remind you about oil slicks and bacteria counts.

Under the pines I strolled behind her, watching my bare feet, and tried once more to think us out of our predicament.

It was, of course, a futile exercise. I am a nasty-problem solver by profession, but in twenty months I hadn't made a dent in this one. And last night the situation had come very near to getting out of hand. When we'd appeased our first and frantic hunger for each other she'd lain quietly in my arms in our Venetian four-poster. ". . . Were you surprised, my darling? Can you guess the reason why I'm two weeks early?"

"There's no guess involved," I said. "You demonstrated. Most convincingly. Of course you also knew how much I wanted you to be here early."

"Steve, I'm such a selfish bitch. Last week I needed you so badly, it was just a matter of, you know, packing a bag and getting on a plane. I didn't even *care* if I'd be inconveniencing you or not." She hesitated briefly, adding: "Or Francisco, come to think of it."

"The general had other plans for you?"

"This weekend and the next, the annual mixed-pairs. They usually let us win it. Actually, he plays very well, but golf has been the farthest from my mind. I told him I was restless." She was not exactly laughing at herself although she managed to appreciate the irony.

"Doesn't it seem to bother him that you're not looking for, let's say, variety?"

"No, Steve. Why should it? I've not changed my dressmak-
er, my doctor, or my travel agent." She laughed then, ruefully.
"Don't you understand? Francisco doesn't worry about you or
me as long as you accept his money."

Or as long as he forgot to wonder if I kept it. Bank records
are opened just as easily as door chains in hotels. Aside from
that uncomfortable possibility, the situation was already worri-
some enough. I found it bearable only because the general was
so evidently hors de combat in his marriage bed.

I said so, not for the first time, and got myself immediately
into trouble. "Steve, I want your child."

". . . That's not very sensible of you."

"I realize that. But I've stopped taking precautions."

It was quite a belt. You can expect a few, of course, over the
years, but this one had me on the canvas. I lay very still, and
took the count, and slowly worked myself up on an elbow and
a knee. "Is your husband dead or dying?"

"*Gracias a Dios*, no. His doctors are extremely proud of
him."

"Then you know very well that this is not to be considered."

"I've considered it." Reclining in the Maja pose beside me
she was catastrophically beautiful. "It's not as unimaginable as
you fear, my darling. We can do it."

"What you are implying," I said slowly, "is that you would
leave your husband. We discussed that in Jamaica, I believe,
almost two years ago."

There had been, even then, too many obstacles. She was
religious in the curiously self-deluding fashion of so many
Catholics who learn how to negotiate with their confessors, and
to whom the form is more important than the substance of a
sin. Money was meaningless to her, and had been all her life;
she'd never cooked a dish, or done her hair, or washed her
stockings. She detested my profession—understandably, per-

haps, but after twenty years I was committed to it.

Then there was the general himself to think about.

"Steve, can't you see? I've gone past caring what he'll do. He'll try to punish us, of course, but we'll just have to cope with that. You've had a lot of practice, haven't you?"

"Enough to know it can't be done."

"What do you mean?"

"There's no such thing as coping with assassination. I'm not even talking about kings or presidents, they're so wide open any crackpot with a gun can burn them down. I'm talking about people with a lot of practice, as you put it. Men or women who don't have to lead a public life, who have made enemies and learned how to protect themselves. They'll normally survive, but not if somebody is willing to spend money. I'm a so-called secret agent. I have seriously inconvenienced perhaps two hundred individuals and half a dozen governments, if any of those bandit gangs behind the Curtain can be called a government. But not enough for any of them to decide they've had it with me. I'd be dead."

"Francisco will spend money," she said calmly. "So will I."

"You haven't got enough."

"Why do you say that? I'm not wealthy like Francisco, or like Marcia Ellis, but my emeralds alone are worth at least two million dollars. And my family will always . . ."

"Let me make my point, please. You just cannot buy security. The U.S. government has tried it a few times, with valuable communist defectors. Plastic surgery and expert vocal coaching. Clinical psychology. Behavioral studies. Fully documented, painstakingly fabricated histories. A Latvian specialist in antimatter physics can be turned into a university librarian from Indiana, and his wife can lose ten years and twenty pounds, and she'll convince you she was born and raised in Brooklyn. They're secure? Not very. No more than a couple of Easter eggs that have been bought and decorated and concealed by a committee of some thirty people. Most of whose identities are known."

She stretched out on her back and stared up at the canopy where smiling nymphs were misbehaving with a faun and with each other. "You don't really believe in cautious living," she said distantly.

"You asked me for a child," I said.

She'd turned away, then, and had covered herself with the top sheet, and refused to notice my attempts at bringing her around. Now, more than twelve hours later, walking through the pine grove on the beach together, she remained aloof, part melancholy, part contemptuous of me.

The worst of it was that I wanted to give in to her.

Not many men feel much of a compulsion about bringing progeny into this world, and very few indeed give any thought to it at my age. But a woman's direct challenge is another matter. Even in a casual or flawed relationship, that challenge strikes a primitive response. When there's a strong attachment, an intense desire to please, it gets about as difficult as self-castration.

I was by no means a stranger to emotional distress. It had been visited on me as far back as the early Thirties, in the days I rode a horse to high school in Los Alamos, New Mexico. Getting a girl in trouble when you don't know any better and you honestly believe that she's the only one for you can hardly qualify as an unusual experience, but it'll stay with you if she drives her father's car over a cliff. Get married while you're still at Texas U. and lose a baby to leukemia, then get drafted and wind up with a Dear Steve, two weeks after you go overseas. Make like a playboy for about ten years until you become hopelessly infatuated with a girl whose navy flyer fiancé was mousetrapped in Mig Alley—she, of course, turns communist and ends up in a sanatorium. Some of the blame is yours: in her presence you shot down the agent who'd corrupted her.

You had to. But you could have hit him in the arm.

You follow through with sixteen years of what had been described last evening as a lot of practice. Then, in Bogotá, Colombia, you fall in love.

Lita de Vargas glanced around at me. We'd come upon the chain link fence that kept the neighbors and the tourists out; the law in Spain prohibits private beaches, but a Spanish judge would ask the plaintiff why he was so anxious to intrude upon a former chief of state. The fence became a palisade of creosoted logs topped with barbed wire and crossed the waterline, continuing for fifty yards into the sea. We turned away from it, leaving the shelter of the pines. The coarse black soil began to scorch our feet.

The little cove faced west and offered morning shade. Its barge load of white sand had been towed in from Portugal and had to be replenished every spring. We stood on it together, watching a big tanker sliding by, one of those quarter-million tonners that seem to pass close enough for you to touch them when they're in a shipping channel half a mile away. "There goes the weekly paycheck of the Sheik of Abadaba," I said soberly. "He actually does buy pretty good protection. On the Persian Gulf." This got me just what it deserved: cold silence. I sat down and hugged my knees. "What are we arguing about? Last night you made me a proposal. I'll accept, of course. As soon as I'm convinced you understand what it involves."

One of her slender, elegantly shapely legs brushed my right shoulder. "Why do you suppose I don't?"

"Maybe you do, but let's make sure, shall we? Assume we go ahead. You'll have to give me a few days to wind up my assignments and clean out my desk, because what I'll be taking on amounts to a new job, full time—I don't mind that, and I don't mind using your money since we wouldn't have a chance without it. So in, say, a week we make our move. First we get

rid of Ana and Jacinto. Not with money, since in my considered judgment they are not corruptible. Also, they know too
much about us. They should really be terminated, but I don't
imagine you'd enjoy that, so I'll settle for just giving them the
slip. And that will be the last time we'll be able to afford any
such compromise."

She watched the tanker, with her leg still touching me.
"I've thought about these things. They make no difference to
me."

"They will, in time." I shook my head and took in a deep
breath. "Please try to form a better picture of the situation.
You are married to a man who sees you as his chattel. He'll
buy anything that'll preserve you or improve you, but when
there's the slightest possibility of losing you he sticks a dinner
fork in you and kills the other guy. Now, for the rest of his
life, maybe ten or fifteen years, you're planning for us to play
hide and seek with him."

"You're not afraid of him," she said. "You couldn't be."

"What are you talking about? You'd better believe it I'm
afraid of him. He can and will hire people who'll make Jacinto
look like a small boy in kindergarten with a water pistol. You
and I might last six months against that kind of talent, or we
just might stay the course by running scared as hell. It would
be a big help if I were less than fifty-four years old, and if you
weren't so goddamned beautiful."

She sat down on her heels, confronting me, prodding my
midriff with one finger. "Look at you. You're just a long-
haired college boy."

"Like Julio Guzmán?"

I'd made her wince. "No, not like him. You'd be the one
who'll graduate from law school next year, or who has been
doing field work for his doctorate in archaeology. You're tall
and lean, and you don't show a wrinkle anywhere. Or you
could pass for an Italian or Spanish engineer or golf pro—any-

thing that kept you out of doors. I've never understood how you sustain that gorgeous tan."

"It isn't very difficult for me. One of my grandmothers was Navajo."

"What's that?"

"A tribe of Indians in New Mexico and Arizona."

She looked mildly startled; I'd have been amused with her in different circumstances. There's a fairly sturdy racial prejudice among the Spanish aristocracy in South America. It never had occurred to her that I might possibly be something of a mongrel. She shook off the punch as if she'd been in training for it. "Steve, the point is that we're both still young. That we can *readjust*."

The point was nothing of the kind. It was that, by ourselves, we might survive if I pulled every trick in the book and made up a few more as we were going. But a pregnant woman isn't very nimble on her feet, and you can't get away from anything at all pushing a baby carriage.

The Carretera de Cadiz had been a narrow, winding ribbon of bad asphalt, two hundred and fifty kilometers long and booby-trapped with washouts, dead man's curves, and rock slides all the way. About four years ago the tourist office in Madrid decided they were losing just a few too many paying customers down the barrancas. They sent in the bulldozers and the cement mixers, and now, if you're in no special hurry, it's a three-hour ride from Málaga around Gibraltar and the Bay of Algeciras, through Tarifa and up the Atlantic coast into the delta of the Guadalquivir.

At a few minutes before nine, that Sunday night, I pulled the little Austin station wagon off the pavement into a convenient lookout area. The mountain view from there was not impressive under a new moon, but the kilometer 180 marker sprang up in my rear-view mirror every time the passing traffic swept its headlights over it. I wasn't in a very happy mood; the past forty-eight hours had strained my charity reserves. There is a certain stage of this where one becomes unreasonable about people who neglect to use their heads.

The U.S. Navy duty officer at Rota had been in that category. Most submariners are on the ball, but this one couldn't seem to make it. Base security was not to be discussed with strangers on the phone. Bat Sullivan, its chief, was not to be disturbed at home, not even by a caller claiming to have gone to school with him. I had hung up and snarled at myself: there was no excuse for my impatience. Monday morning would do just as well. Leon de Bas could certainly not be persuaded to show up before tomorrow night.

A motor scooter sputtered off the highway, crunched into the gravel of the lookout, and pulled up behind me. There is something oddly inappropriate about two large policemen sharing such a vehicle, but it's a common sight in Spain. Of course such men are not on duty; they're just using their own transportation. These wore winged black leather hats and moss green uniforms. Legs spread, thumbs hooked into their pistol belts, they stood surveying me. They were exactly what I had in mind, two brawny, middle-aged, impassive Guardias Civiles interested in a little medium-dishonest moonlighting.

"*Muy buenas.* You are the Americano who requires an escort for his friend?" The spokesman had a gray mustache to match the heavy local accent I had heard that morning on the phone. He saw my nod and grunted, satisfied. "Where does he wish to go, this friend of yours?"

"He has strange preferences. He likes submarines and those who sail in them."

"That is unusual."

"It is. But let us humor him. Tomorrow I shall make arrangements for his visit to a certain naval base. Then I shall point him out to you, and you will take him there. I would suggest you rent a car."

They exchanged glances. "That will be expensive. There are buses."

"It will be my privilege to pay for a good car. A big one. My friend eats too much. Also, his body does not smell agreeable."

They didn't question me. I had been recommended to them by Antonio Molina, who outranked them in the service of the government. "The automobile will cost twelve hundred pesetas, señor."

"Very well. And for yourselves?"

We settled for six thousand, which is just over a hundred dollars—close to a month's salary for them. They were part-time policemen, Andalusian farmers with a few months' training but with twenty years or so of manhandling the small-time crooks and gypsy thieves who were their normal prey. Moreover, they had private telephones. I took the numbers, parted with a thousand pesetas by way of earnest money, and received their solemn, iron-calloused handshakes in return before they got back on their scooter and buzzed off, the little Vespa almost disappearing under their collective bulk.

I drove the few kilometers back to the Villa Calayán. The covered patio was festive with Chinese lanterns lighted by insect-repellent bulbs. Ana Gómez was serving appetizers while her husband tended bar; Lita, reclining on a deck chair, seemed to be about two Gibsons up on me.

"Darling, where *have* you been?"

"Attending to my business."

"Were you?" She looked convincingly offended. But we were just playing to our audience. She knew perfectly well that my time was not my own, and that it might not have been even if she'd come in two weeks later. "If you must see other people, can't you manage to be here for cocktails? I don't like to drink alone."

"Then don't."

She threw her empty glass at me, not very hard. I moved my head out of its way; the crystal tinkled on the patio tiles. Jacinto was already coming over to us with his tray. I waved him off and said, in English, "You don't need another one, and I shall do without. We'll have the '59 Dom Pérignon with dinner." When she started to protest I touched two fingers to her lips. She tried to bite them, saw my grin, and broke up into laughter, musically, while behind us Ana Gómez quietly swept up the shards.

It's not impossible to buy good beef in Spain, just difficult— about as difficult as buying a good English cup of coffee. We spent time and effort getting through our tournedos. The fish course that preceded it, and the champagne, had put us in sufficiently good humor to stand up to it. But she was worrying about me. "You aren't mixed up in anything the Spanish government might disapprove of, are you?"

"I suppose they might. Although there are no Spanish interests involved."

"What do you mean?"

Her quick concern was understandable. We'd made no progress solving our own disconcerting problems, and here I was carelessly admitting to the possibility of getting into trouble with the country that supplied us sanctuary, and with its notoriously disagreeable political police. I said: "There's someone in Tangier who wants a favor. He expects to hear from me about it in the morning. I shall phone and tell him that it's all arranged."

"What sort of favor?"

"Well, he wants to go to Belgium for some reason. I'm to

lay on transportation and facilities."

She frowned at me. "Why doesn't he just buy a plane ticket?"

"Because he's not exactly, shall we say, persona grata."

"So you'll have to smuggle him in," she said scornfully.

"The circumstances are unusual."

"So much so that you can't discuss them with me?"

We were actually squabbling like a married couple. I said yes, of course we could discuss them, but they wouldn't make particularly pleasant dinner table conversation, and they certainly weren't for the servants' ears, regardless of how little English they might understand. I'd had my doubts in that respect about Jacinto for some time, who chose that very moment to return and bow over my chair. "*Teléfono para usted, señor.*"

I raised an eyebrow at him, bowed to Lita, and walked back into the house. The phone receiver under the west staircase in the living room was off the hook. It hissed at me like a small, angry animal; there was a radio carrier wave on it, distorting Marcia Ellis's vibrant soprano. "Steve, are you there? Speak up, please, I can't hear you!"

Radio meant the *Miss Virginia*, at sea. I felt both eyebrows go and said impassively: "Now you can hear me. So can quite a lot of people."

"Yes, dear, I shall be discreet. I've done you a big favor and I want you to be properly appreciative. We're tying up in Puerto Banus in about an hour, and we have on board my guest of honor of last Friday night."

It was a good, stiff jolt. Puerto Banus was the nearest yacht harbor, almost in spitting distance, and last Friday's guest of honor was, of course, His would-be Royal Majesty Carol the Third, with whom I had intended to do business next week in Tangier. Certainly I had no use for him at all here in Marbella.

Marcia Ellis knew this very well. I checked my watch: almost eleven. "Thanks for calling," I said pleasantly enough. "I'll see you in an hour, and we'll talk about it, shall we?"

"Listen," she said quickly. "Please don't be surprised if you should run into the kids."

"You mean the Strawberries? All *four* of them?"

"Steve, dear, I know you told the boys to go by air. But they showed up at the last minute, just as we were casting off —they'd missed their plane after they had a tiff with the Moroccan customs people. Not about you-know-what, but it seems there was some money they'd forgotten to declare. I couldn't leave them *stranded*, could I?"

"What about their luggage?"

". . . I guess they have it with them. Surely you can do something about that in the morning?"

"Marcia dear," I said, "do you remember what I told you yesterday at lunch?"

She did, of course; she was about as feebleminded as a ferret. I had warned her quite specifically against letting drugs be brought aboard. But she would have some sort of an excuse. It would have happened fast, under embarrassing conditions, possibly before an audience she didn't care to entertain, and probably with the girl Valerie in tears, demanding to be left behind with her companions. And in Spain there would be Steve dear, who could be expected to do something about it in the morning.

If he had the vaguest notion what to do, which he did not. I said so, but she didn't even hear me. She was chattering right on about what sounded inauspiciously like something else.

"I missed that. *Who'd* you say begged for a ride and wants to see me?"

"Oh, you've met him. He was at my party Friday night. Sven Wahlstrom brought him, they were in some sort of a transaction with each other. He's a big, fat Dutchman from South Africa or something. I'm afraid I can't think of his name."

I said I could. "You turned him down, of course."

"No, dear, I didn't. He's on board. The kids like him. Also, he said he has a proposition for you."

I took three deep breaths and said: "All right, that's fine. Now you must do exactly as I tell you. See this man immediately. Mention to him that you've spoken with me, that I'm interested, and that I'll reserve a room for him. The Atalaya Park Hotel, I'll have them send a taxi, he's to go there straight away and I'll arrange a meeting with him in the morning. If that doesn't suit him, tell him that you're sorry but that you can't put him up on *Miss Virginia*—be very firm, if necessary have the stewards show him off the gangway. Is that understood?"

"No, dear, it isn't, but I'll do it."

"Very good. As for the Strawberries, they're not to be allowed ashore. Not even Valerie. Not until I've made other dispositions. I imagine they will see the logic of that, but if not, you'll have to have them locked up in their cabins. Separately would be best."

The ship-to-shore wave sizzled in my ear for a few seconds before Marcia laughed on it, uneasily. "I guess you're right."

"Get on with it, then, and I'll see you shortly after you tie up. As soon as I can make it."

She hung up and I flashed back the local operator, got through to the desk at the hotel and booked a room and transportation from the harbor for Leon de Bas. Then I rang one of the two numbers that had been provided by the motor scooter Guardia Civil. It answered promptly; Spaniards never seem to go to bed at night. I said my friend had changed his plans and was arriving early. This would obviously involve a certain inconvenience, which would afford a further five hundred pesetas.

After that, I got the Rota duty officer back on the line. This time I didn't fool around with him. There is a signal that emerged from the communications foul-up at Pearl Harbor in the early morning of December 7, 1941. You're not supposed to use it without hostile spaceships actually coming down on top of you, but if you do it gets results. Commander William P. "Bat" Sullivan, USN, came on fast and strong. "Harvester? If I know you, you can tell me what we scored against Kentucky in the Cotton Bowl in '38."

"We've never played Kentucky," I said coldly. "We beat LSU in '38, by 27-21. You threw the winning pass."

He cleared the gravel from his throat, or most of it. "Okay, I know you. You're a spook in Jimmy Dexter's circus. Where do you get off pitching the Doomsday code at my OD?"

"I had to make him listen to me, Bat," I said. "Bug me some other time about it. People have been squaring out on me all day. I've got a customer for you, a nasty one. Brussels has tried to put the arm on him for years."

"Why me, buddy? Just turn him over to the Dons. They'll fix his radiator."

"No. He's clean in Spain."

That got a snort from him. There's no such animal as a clean communist in Spain. But if his passport is in order, and he isn't into anything, he'll be allowed to spend his money. Extradition means you show your files and wait about six months. The Spaniards aren't in NATO. They would like to be.

Bat Sullivan was saying: "Let's assume I go along with you on this, for old times' sake, how do you wanna play it?"

I explained, and he considered, briefly, and supplied instructions. We exchanged the customary insults and hung up. Lita was sulking over coffee and liqueurs when I rejoined her on the patio. I had a little less than half an hour to spare, and used it carefully with her, but when she learned that I was on my way again we almost had ourselves a real confrontation. "You can't be *serious*!"

"I'm afraid I am."

"Where did you get this horrible idea that you can just walk out like that, on any woman you're supposed to care about? Your charming *grandmother* from *Arizona?*"

Racially uptight I'm not, but I was fairly strongly tempted all the same to put her down. Most likely that was what she wanted, so I merely shook my head. "It's an emergency."

"If you could know how much I hate that ghastly job of yours. . . ." She trembled with emotion, clinging to my arm. "You said this ruffian you're to help sneak into Belgium isn't even due until tomorrow."

"I was wrong about that." It seemed hardly practical to go into detail. But Marcia Ellis's predicament was something else; I didn't want her to find out about that later. "*Miss Virginia* is docking here in twenty minutes."

"Oh?"

"She's got a bomb aboard. Not the explosive type, but troublesome enough."

Lita released my arm, sat down, looked up at me through lowered lashes. "How long will you be?"

"As long as necessary."

We were back on solid ground. She moved her lips for a goodbye kiss. "Hurry, please."

The Atalaya Park Hotel sprawls over twenty acres, but its main pavilion has a central registration desk. At midnight there was still plenty of tourist traffic in the lobby. I had bought a newspaper from the hall porter and was using it, as secret agents must, to make myself invisible. My hired confederates were sipping their espressos at our distant-corner table. They did not look out of place. They wore respectable black suits, clean shirts, and knitted ties, and they were freshly shaved; they might be politicians from Madrid, or local businessmen studying their trade. The bulging muscles and the austere soldier profiles could not harm this picture. Millions of Spaniards in their middle age would fit right in, marching with

Cortez or Pizarro after Inca gold.

Their rented car was in the parking lot, a Seat taxi they had taken over from its owner-driver for the night. I had already paid them off. "You understand, señores, that my friend is dangerous? He may attempt to harm you. He will certainly try to escape."

This earned a flat-eyed stare from both of them. They were about as much impressed as if I'd told them that the trunk I'd asked them to deliver might be just a little heavy.

"*Bueno*, he will be in Cadiz in two hours. There can be no difficulty in this. Not if the Americanos meet us there."

Bat Sullivan had promised me a launch that would be waiting at the foot of Pier 14, off the Paseo Maritimo and an easy run across the bay to Rota. I was fairly sure I could rely on him. "They will be there."

"Then we shall need no more than that you point him out to us, your friend."

A man came off the elevators, crossed the lobby, passed within a few feet from our table and moved on into the television lounge. I ducked behind my newspaper at his approach, because he, too, was big and grossly overweight. But he was in his thirties, Scandinavian or German by appearance, and he took no notice of us; and just then Leon de Bas came waddling in behind the doorman and two pages carrying his luggage. I said sharply: "Watch the desk, señores, *por favor*. My friend is checking in."

They looked and nodded, and the one with the hard gray mustache gave me a shrug. "Why do you trouble hiding from him, señor?"

"If he sees me, he will realize that this is not a regular arrest. In that event, he will cause serious complications." I'd been in a similar position once myself, in Italy, and even with my terrible Italian had managed to arouse suspicion in too many people within fifty yards, too quickly for the comfort of the phony carabinieri who were trying to walk off with me under the opposition's personal direction.

"*Bueno*, we shall take him from his room." The gray mustache curled in a sneer. "There is no further need to incommode yourself, señor."

They were dismissing me, convinced of my timidity. I didn't mind; the game plan was as good as I could improvise on such short notice. At the desk, Leon de Bas had finished registering. He looked tired and irritable as he followed the chasseur who had his key. Of course I knew why he was here: he'd made it clear enough that his instructions were to block my trafficking with the Rumanians. When he found out that Marcia had taken them in tow for me, he'd evidently thought it best to keep in touch.

I didn't fold my newspaper until the elevator doors had closed.

The little Austin purred away from the hotel with me and covered the two miles to Puerto Banus. It was getting on to one A.M., but the big yacht harbor still blazed under its sodium arcs and crackled with activity. More than a hundred of the slips were occupied, and more than half of them had something going—you could almost lean against the tide of stereo flamenco rock. The customs booth was closed, but at the gate a single aduana officer lounged on the bench, smoking a big cigar and casually returning my salute. Almost directly over him loomed *Miss Virginia*'s prow, a huge white hatchet blade. Her fifteen hundred tons of lovingly converted warship reared above the common herd of ketches, sloops, and ocean-going power boats. Her gangway watch gave me the British fishy eye and stopped me cold until a steward brought out Marcia herself, in negligee.

The air-conditioned living quarters of the owner's suite glowed with black antelope and polished cherrywood. She sat demurely on her ankles on the couch, watching me pace her fifty thousand dollars' worth of Persian carpet. "Steve dear, aren't you *grateful?*"

"I don't know," I said. "Let me be sure I've got this straight. You're telling me that Yuri Franklin called you around noon and claimed she had to talk with me. You thought it better not to mention where I could be reached. You pumped her carefully and learned of something to my disadvantage, namely, that His Majesty and entourage were leaving for the south of France. You knew I was supposed to meet them in Tangier next week, and you suspected that it was a little more important than I had explained to you. Where'd you get that idea?"

"How could I miss?" Her smile deplored my innocence. "Yuri's a pretty thing, but she's so *mercenary.* If she's interested in you it must be because you're paying her, and I don't think you're into that just yet. Not even with *young* women. So you're paying her for something else, which means you're something else besides a writer. As I've known for a long time," she added with a shrug.

I brushed that off with an impatient gesture. Cover can be terribly important, of course, sometimes to the point where you stake life and limb on it, but in this instance it was just a matter of convenience—a courtesy of sorts to all concerned, a form of stock in trade. I was a writer and could prove it, didn't even need to prove it since I'd been established in the literary business since 1946. "All right," I said. "I'm grateful. It was kind of you to help. You told Yuri you'd do something about it. Then you got Prince Sturza on the phone."

"He's difficult, you know," said Marcia. "He *criticized* me. I should realize it was presumptuous of me to invite His Majesty to be my guest at Antibes for a week or two. Of course it just so happened they were going down there on affairs of state —was I aware of this somehow? I told him no, of course I wasn't, but how awfully *fortuitous*, and why didn't we all just pack up right now and ride on down on *Miss Virginia?* He hemmed and hawed a lot, and turned me down, but in five minutes he got back to me, accepting. And so here we are. D'you want to join the party, you and Lita?''

She knew very well I didn't, but that I might have to. I stood looking at her with my back against the paneled bulkhead between two enormous portholes; she was smiling for me, her indulgent smile that said I was a good boy and deserved her patronage, but that I really should wake up one of these days. "Affairs of state," I said. "Such as?"

"Haven't a clue, dear. Yuri should."

I said I would ask Yuri in the morning. "How long can you keep them here on ice for me?"

"Not long, dear."

"No, I guess not. Please tell Yuri I'll be at the Atalaya Park around eleven, on the terrace. Plan to sail tomorrow night at dinner time. I should be able to get organized by then. Meanwhile it'll be necessary to do something pretty drastic to those hippies you picked up."

"Such as?"

"Don't get defiant with me, Marcia. If the local customs pull a snap search on you, you are dead. They can seize *Miss Virginia* and put her in the Spanish Navy. They can drag you through their courts for years. You'll wind up six or seven million dollars out of pocket, and the newspapers'll have a ball with you as long as you're around. You lock the boys into their cabins?"

"It wasn't necessary. They're asleep. I told them that you'd, well, you know, work something out with them tomorrow."

"Can't be done. They take the stuff ashore, they'll be arrested, it comes out you brought them. I'd suggest you put them off just before sailing, but the Dons might send a chopper after you to stop you in their territorial waters. Certainly you couldn't come back in. Not ever. They might even try to extradite. They love to prove they're a democracy. By jumping on celebrities."

She thought it over. "What's the answer?"

"Very simple. Confiscate the junk and dump it in the harbor. Give the kids their plane fare home and put them off. Right now. I'll handle it for you."

"No, Steve."

"Oh, come now, Marcia. You've got to. Either that, or schlepp the whole kit and caboodle back to Tangier, where they might not even let it in. You can't take it to France. Americans carrying drugs are lucky not to get the guillotine in France."

She shook her head, obstinately. "I have friends in France."

"You have one right here in this room," I said, exasperated with her. But it was no use, of course. When there is that much money, common sense isn't abandoned—just suspended every now and then. She got her bare feet back under her, rose off the couch, and padded over to me. She grasped hold of my lapels and tried to shake me by them. She looked forty, sure of herself, and as sexy as Maureen O'Hara in her better days. I didn't need Maureen O'Hara, but I'm not exactly unsusceptible or antisocial.

From the doorway to the bedroom, the girl Valerie said sleepily: "Hey, Marsh, I'm *lonesome*." She wore lilac nylon babydoll pajamas, frilly ones that put another five or ten pounds on her. But she'd actually had a shower and a shampoo, fairly recently. She rubbed her eyes, saw us, and looked vaguely puzzled. "Oh! Don't I know you?"

"No, Miss Gardner, you don't know me," I said soberly enough, releasing Marcia, who appeared to be amused with me.

There was a powder room for guests. I wandered into it, scrubbed the lipstick off, and carefully, censoriously surveyed myself. When I came out, the living room was empty but the bedroom door remained ajar. I cleared my throat and mentioned loudly that I would be leaving now but would return tomorrow sometime around noon.

Behind the bedroom door, Marcia moaned as if in sudden agony. I hesitated, turning on my heels, and heard Valerie Gardner say: "Oh wow, what're you *doing?*" and the answering moan, not at all expressing pain this time. I shrugged and turned away, and left the owner's suite and *Miss Virginia.*

MARBELLA, MONDAY, JULY 19.

Antonia Molina called me from his airport office just as I was leaving for the Atalaya Park Hotel. He sounded quite as cheerful as on Sunday morning, but not quite so casual. "*Hola, amigo Esteban*! What's happening?"

"Not much," I said. "I should've called you back last night, Antonio. But I was busy, and I didn't get the word myself in time. Those customers I had for you seem to have missed their plane."

"You mentioned three of them," he carefully reminded me. "Their names were Michael C. McGowan, Basil Nichols, and George Johnson, is that not correct?"

In different circumstances this might have been pretty funny. He had checked the airline manifest, of course, and spotted three no-shows on it: the passport names of Mick and Croup and Hero Pud. The trouble was that now, if he felt so inclined, he probably could put a tracer on these names. When people miss their planes they usually manage to find other transportation.

That would not suit Marcia, and it wouldn't suit me even if she weren't a friend of mine. Then, on the other hand, there really isn't very good cooperation between customs officers across most borders, and Morocco doesn't make the Spanish most-respected-nations list. I said I had another set of names but that these might be aliases. "Let me work on this for you, Antonio. I'll need another day or so."

"*Muy bien, querido*." It was fine with him, but when a Spaniard calls you that, watch out. Used between men, *querido* carries the same overtones of skepticism that a Londoner can put in the word luv. I said I'd do the best I could, *querido*, and he thanked me, wished me luck, and bade me *adiós*. With Spanish tactfulness he did not ask if I'd been pleased with the persuasive-escort service he'd referred to me the day before.

It turned out fairly soon that I had need of all these charming sentiments.

Miss Yuri Franklin, garbed in classical white sharkskin and high-platform sandals, strolled across the Atalaya terrace to my table and bestowed a dazzling smile on me from under the wide brim of her black Andalusian castor hat. We shared a padded swing under a gaudy parasol and sipped our sherries with a dish of salted peanuts and green olives on the side, just like a tourist couple on the morning of a big night at the bull-fights. "Are you pleased with me, Steve Harvester?"

Of course I was supposed to be. She had delivered. That is something you don't take for granted, in this business or any other business. I hadn't even formally agreed to pay her yet.

"Suppose you tell me why we're off to France," I said.

Her smile was losing candlepower. "Carol hasn't told me."

"Hasn't he?"

I sounded disappointed rather than incredulous. She put a hand on my knee, squeezed me, and said very earnestly: "I could've made him tell me, but I didn't think you'd want me to. It might've taken too much time, and the important thing was after all that we were going."

"Didn't you remind him that he had a date with me this week?"

"He brought it up himself. He said you'd keep." She

laughed, not necessarily with me, a tinkly little geisha laugh.

"Come on, Miss Franklin. What's in France that wouldn't keep? I might accept that you weren't told, but please don't ask me to believe you didn't manage to find out."

"Oh, I can guess," she said, almost judiciously reasonable, and I caught a glimpse of the young Stanford undergraduate she'd been just a few years ago, discussing politics or anthropology on a campus bench. "There *has* been talk for quite a while. About a politicians' delegation from back home in Bucarest." She watched me look disinterested; she knew very well I wasn't. "Carol has a stepbrother, you know. His name is Michael, and he lives near Cannes. They're trying to play off one against the other."

I said I knew about the stepbrother, but that I couldn't read a Bucarest approach. "Nothing comes out of there without the Ceauşescu government's approval. They're supposed to like the Chinese better than the Russians, but they're *communists*, Miss Franklin."

"Does that really matter so much?"

"If the monarchy is ever reinstalled, it will. They'll be turned off."

She thought about that. "But the Reds aren't always incompatible or hostile, are they? In Cambodia they support Prince Sihanouk. And in Rumania itself, didn't the Russians restore Michael to the throne, right after World War II?"

"Yes, for a little while," I said. "Until he started talking about free elections. He was very young."

"I'm almost sure that there's a delegation coming," she said stubbornly.

She could be right, I thought. But it would have to be clandestine, and it would consist of peasant politicians from the provinces. If so, that suited me, of course, provided there would not arise a situation in which everybody had his hand out, although I was used to this and would, if necessary, deal with it. The only thing that bothered me just then was a vague sense of trouble: something out of line, something with an offensive smell—and that was it, a whiff of body acid, a familiar taint that should have been removed more than a hundred miles away. Yet it was right here on this terrace, somewhere close behind, quite close enough to overcome the heady fragrance of Arpège worn by the girl beside me on the swing.

I glanced around, casually, with an effort to conceal my disbelief. Leon de Bas was bearing down on us, still ten or fifteen feet away, and hideously naked but for outsize bathing shorts and rubber sandals. Both his arms were out to us, and he was actually favoring us with what I was forced to recognize as an ingratiating smile. "Good morning and good morning, my dear friends. Are you well met by chance or by design?"

Yuri, who after all had little cause to be surprised by his appearance, merely raised one of her shapely eyebrows at him. I came to my reasonably steady feet and managed without visible reluctance to shake hands. The exercise was not unlike squeezing a greasy pillow. "On my way to call your room," I lied convincingly enough.

"You've news for me, my boy?" He seemed entirely unaware of anything at all amiss.

I said I did, and he looked pleased with me and told me he'd be on the beach, at my disposal. When he'd waddled out of earshot Yuri, frowning after him, suggested that he must be very rich. I shrugged and said he had that reputation, but that I would hardly recommend her trying to confirm it.

"I like money," she said coolly. "But not that much." She seemed glad to put the matter from her mind. "Will you be sailing with us to Antibes tonight?" she carefully inquired.

I said there was a possibility of it, and was rewarded with a sidelong, frankly speculative glance before she rose, conventionally smiling. She explained that she would have to visit the boutiques at the hotel as an excuse for having come ashore. "If you should not be joining us, Steve Harvester, how shall we keep in touch? Through Marcia?''

''For the present, yes.''

She touched my lips with Arpège-scented fingertips and walked away from me, her legs provocative yet moving with controlled decorum. I strolled after her into the lobby, found a phone, and used my credit card.

Bat Sullivan, in Rota, sounded much more curious than exasperated. ''Looks like you fucked up this time, old buddy.''

''Does it?''

''Yessir, that it does. We met those Spanish cops you hired, last night, and they produced your man. They'd been a little rough on him, and it turned out he didn't have much English and no Spanish, so we made no sense with him until the medics worked him over. Then we got to him, but Brussels doesn't want him. He's a German stockbroker from Regensburg, Bavaria. We checked him out like there was no tomorrow.''

You can't really afford a sense of humor in this business. I made a noise intended to convey embarrassment. It served to cover up the chuckle that had forced itself on me. I was a victim of the leading Spanish national trait of character, a form of lofty self-respect. No Spaniard ever double checks on anything —the notion that he might just possibly be making a mistake cannot occur to him, although he doesn't consciously believe himself infallible—accuse him of it and he'll be offended, for the accusation is itself in conflict with this *altivez* of his.

There had been two fat men last night.

Bat Sullivan was saying: ''Now you realize, old buddy, that this lad could grab us where it hurts.''

I didn't think so. Tourists are like Santa Claus, beloved by everybody, but the minute one gets into trouble over anything at all the lid comes down. The local cops don't understand him or respect him. Local lawyers just want to milk him. Government bureaus set up to serve him only hand out maps and sightseeing brochures. His consul views him as a dumbo and a drunk who brought whatever happened on himself.

"Just turn him loose, Bat. Let him call his wife. Buy him a bus ticket back to Marbella."

"She's in Regensburg."

"Oh?"

"Yessir, you fucked up all right," he reassured me. "But not real bad. NATO's not interested in your man, but the Bavarian authorities are looking for him. He took off with something like two million marks in customers' securities, last month."

Leon de Bas had tipped the beach attendant and had been equipped with mattress, back rest, parasol, and with an ashtray for his arrogant cigar. He'd wrapped a towel, turban-fashion, over his bald skull; he looked like an obese but powerfully muscled woman. Perspiration dribbled down his bull neck into a confluence that became a tunnel in the cleavage of his jutting breasts, then spread into a double flow when parted at the midriff by his paunch. He'd put wet cotton pads over both eyelids as if he were anxious to avoid spoiling his tan with sunglasses.

But he was well aware of my approach. "You are still tampering with these deplorable Rumanians, my dear 'Arvestair."

"That's right."

"I thought we understood each other. This will not be tolerated."

"Sorry about that," I said.

Such warnings had been given to me by assorted members of the opposition for some twenty years. One day, of course, somebody would proceed to prove something to me, and this might be the day. I looked down at de Bas, standing upwind from him about three feet away, feeling the sand trickle into my moccasins, and struggling with myself to find a sensible solution of the problem he presented. It was quite a problem, I was under no illusions about that. If he believed it necessary, he would try to turn me off, in somewhat the same manner he'd put down Sven Wahlstrom.

He'd be just as likely to try using Lita as a handle on me. It occurred to me that I might put Jacinto Gómez in the ring with him. But the result would be a little messy, and not really predictable.

"Americans," de Bas was saying, "always seem to me incapable of serious discussion. Not even your leaders in their public speeches can restrain themselves from making so-called wisecracks or from sounding insincere."

I said that might be so, but that most Europeans had no sense of humor. "Get this straight. Where the Rumanians are concerned, you people are in no position to butt in. Taking me out won't do a bit of good, of course, since there are twenty others like me. Take out Carol and you'll turn ten million hostile peasants into active revolutionaries. Lay on the Red Army and you've lost another Warsaw Pact ally and tied up ten divisions. That'll suit us fine, and the Chinese as well."

"I don't make policy," he told me coldly. "I just carry out instructions." He removed the cotton pad on his left eye and fixed me with a baleful stare, which isn't easily achieved when you are on your back and looking up. He made a creditable job of it, but when my knees didn't start shaking he put back the pad over his eye. "You've talked with Brussels, my dear fellow?"

"Let's assume I have."

"And they agreed, of course, to my proposal. But not in good faith. You thereupon explained that I must be protected. By two eligible hostages, such as Señora Vargas and yourself."

I said: "Now look, de Bas, whatever makes you think that we'd go into anything like that? Why should we care that much about this Dancing Dog of yours? You claim that it's a conduit into the U.S., but they come pretty cheap. You people haven't had much trouble getting almost anything across our borders in, like, fifty years."

"Only when very careful timing and complete security were not required, my boy." He blindly stabbed at me with his cigar to emphasize the point.

That was more like it. "Timing and security? For what? Don't tell me the Politburo is on that kick again!"

Way back in '49, when the Berlin blockade was getting nowhere, good old Uncle Joe himself had come up with the brilliant idea of smuggling an atomic bomb right into Washington. As legend has it, he persuaded everybody in the mob from Molotov on down to go along. Of course they didn't manage to keep that one secret, not even in Moscow; when the coast guard and the border patrol promptly started checking everything bulky with a Geiger counter, they gave up on it.

But the event acquired a lasting fame in the intelligence community as Operation Borschthead. After more than twenty years, Leon de Bas had little difficulty recognizing my allusion to it. "Don't be facetious, 'Arvestair. There were no missiles in those days."

"There are now. Who needs timing and security?" No answer. "Oh, come off it," I said irritably. "You're the one who approached Brussels with this, and you want a hell of a big favor in return." No comment on that either—he just lay there in the sun, perspiring copiously, reeking like a stoat. I didn't altogether blame him. If he really had something to offer, he could lose it all by dropping one too many hints. "All right, forget the deal," I said and started to walk off.

His fruity tenor bent my ear before I'd made three yards. "Suppose I tell you what is to be carried in this conduit, my dear fellow."

I swung round, confronting him again. "That's up to you. If you're not very sure that Section Six'll buy it, don't embarrass me with it." But he'd already taken off both eye pads and was studying our entourage. We were enjoying reasonable privacy; most of the other guests preferred the pool lawn to the beach. Our closest neighbors were a Spanish family preoccupied with half a dozen lively kids.

"Come closer, 'Arvestair."

I shook my head and took a single step to humor him. Conspiracies don't benefit from obvious close quarters; neither would my nose.

"Let's have it."

". . . B. W. material."

The leer he offered me was sinister enough. I winced with disappointment. "Try again."

"Surely you understand, my body? B-biological. W-warfare. Very nasty stuff. Brussels will have to sit up and take notice, don't you see."

The only thing I saw, only too clearly, was that his condition—physical or mental, perhaps both—must be a great deal worse than had been evident until just then. This didn't much reduce the problem he presented; after all, an invalid can cause a lot of harm as long as he is ambulant. But problem or no problem, I had had it with him. "Yes, I'm sure that Brussels will be terribly impressed," I said. "If you'll excuse me now, I'll get right after them with it. Don't even breathe until we let you know."

"You don't believe me?" Much to my surprise he merely put the pads back on his eyelids and relaxed. "You will regret this error in evaluation, 'Arvestair," he told me almost placidly. "You also will regret the consequences if that Wall Street clique of yours persists in subsidizing the Rumanians." I shrugged and started to walk out on him again, but he had one more shot left in his locker. "Incidentally, may I inquire how you propose to handle Mrs. Ellis's predicament?"

". . . Care to be a little more specific?"

"My dear boy, must I? Did you imagine I was unaware that *Miss Virginia* carries contraband?"

"Listen to me, de Bas," I said between my teeth. "Here's some bad news for you. You've only been in this unpleasant trade of ours for about ten years, and you've run up a reputation as a butcher. Fortunately for you that's not my concern, but if you bother any of my friends I'll personally hang your carcass from a meat hook."

He'd put up one of his pudgy hands. "Spare me your evil temper, 'Arvestair. You've quite misunderstood me."

"Have I?"

"Mrs. Ellis has my sympathy. I spoke severely to young Basil Nichols when he boasted to me of the misbehavior of his friends. Will you permit me to adjust the matter? As a favor to my hostess and to you."

I stared at him, or rather at the pads over his eyes. "How would you go about it?"

"Very simply. By removing the corpus delicti and arranging for its safe delivery in New York City." It was almost an amusing situation. He was actually offering to do the job I had pretended to take on. I made a noise somewhere between a chuckle and a snort, which he preferred to misinterpret. "Not to worry, my dear fellow. I can do it. There will be no risk involved for anyone."

"That's very kind of you, de Bas," I said. "But speaking for both Mrs. Ellis and myself, it seems to me we'd better not impose on you."

On the short drive from the hotel back to the Villa Calayán I took about two minutes, reconsidering. Something had to be done about the blowsy Belgian. He was a sick man, but he was much too dangerous to keep around.

No thought of summoning my private Guardia Civil back into action came to me. You don't pick up your arrows in this game if you can help it, and in any case I'd have a job talking Bat Sullivan into his part of it; he'd made that clear enough to me. Of course I could call Brussels after all. But Section Six would take its time, investigating, contemplating, deprecating. If I'd had something for them they could have fried in butter and served up for breakfast, that might have worked out, but as it was I couldn't even prove it was Leon de Bas who'd put their man away. Or offer them a reasonable explanation of the fact that Captain Wahlstrom had tried unsuccessfully to visit me, a minute or two before he was killed, last Friday night.

I couldn't give them Dancing Dog, since it was very obvious and very crude disinformation. Speaking properly it did not even qualify as such, because the concept of disinformation involves plausibility. B.W. has not been plausible for many years. It never really was, of course, but you can't blame the boys in the white coats for playing with it, or the generals for worrying about it, for a while.

As long as there is going to be war the business of military scientists is to design the weapons that will win it, and it's pretty tempting to come up with something to destroy the enemy before he can be sure that it is being used on him. When it turns out that such a weapon can be easily produced, at small expense, some people will get terribly excited. They may either see themselves as masters of the universe, or they may see the opposition taking charge as such. It takes a little time, say thirty years or so, for everybody to cool down and listen to the voice of common sense.

For about twenty million dollars, any country with a medical laboratory to its name can cultivate a germ or virus that will kill and kill and kill, without affecting those protected by the proper vaccine or by something like a narrow-spectrum, specially devised antibiotic. At that point, we only need to solve three little problems. We must somehow manage to inoculate our population and our allies, secretly. We'd better think of something to contend with up to two and a half billion cadavers, enemy and neutral, most of them presumably unburied. Then there's the unhappy possibility of a mutation in the weapon's biological component.

If that happens, there will be no problems anymore, for us or anybody else, because such a mutation will invalidate our own initial immunity.

Nobody minds getting a little pregnant, naturally. Such as by dusting the other fellow's countryside with crop-destroying organisms. Or by carefully infecting troops in territory we don't want to occupy ourselves for now—with something we can always handle if we have to. Nothing ostentatious, little scrub typhus or something. But what everybody has been seeing eye to eye about for quite a while now is that nobody'll ever try B.W. for real, not with the big bad people-eater bug. The kind that would have to be smuggled through a conduit. With close timing and complete security.

So that still left me with a hostile and obnoxious Russian agent on my hands.

I put the little Austin in the car port, walked across the croquet lawn under the stately cedars, and ascended to the patio. It was just a few minutes after noon; the sun stood high, scorching the tile mosaic under my lightly sandaled feet. Ana Gómez, superintending two young local village girls at work cleaning the windows of the living room, gave me her customary flat-eyed stare. I managed to ignore her with a smile, as usual, and mounted the east staircase to the master suite.

In the boudoir, a recently demolished breakfast tray had been abandoned on the bed. Lita, reclining on a canvas pallet on the private terrace, made a mouth for me to kiss. Her tan was milk chocolate-luscious, with the markings left by her bikini that had been in evidence two days ago now almost gone. "Must I try to blush, my darling? You look *terribly* dressed up."

I said that could be remedied, acted accordingly, and stretched out on the second pallet, wearing only sunglasses. She got up on her knees beside me and put oil on me, which I don't need except as the excuse for a massage. I didn't really need that either, not just then.

"I shouldn't even be here."

"What do you mean?"

Last night I'd explained Marcia's indiscretion to her, without mentioning my Balkan troubles or Leon de Bas. "The situation isn't very well in hand. I worked on it this morning, but the needle just keeps skipping grooves."

"Oh, *she'll* come to her senses," Lita said impatiently. "You told her what to do about the drugs."

"I didn't tell her anything she didn't know."

"You really think those kids can make her take them to New York?"

"No, she'll get tired of them," I said. "But it turns out that she has other people with her. People from Tangier she has invited to her house on the Riviera. Do you want to go?"

The hands rubbing Ambre Solaire into my back withdrew. "Steve, why?" I told her why, and she considered for about ten seconds. "Must you stick to this abominable job of yours when we're together?"

I prevented myself from reminding her that her arrival two weeks early had something to do with it. "The job isn't as bad as that. It did bring you and me together. It kept half a magazine of submachine gun slugs out of your hair two years ago."

"You callous, evil-minded Indian!" She slapped me on the buttocks, hard. "If I weren't so preposterously mad about you . . . Very well, then, we shall go to France with Marcia. Just for a few days, to let you bribe her sordid friends." More suntan oil splashed on my lower back.

One little thing like that leads to another. It was almost three o'clock before I got around to picking up the phone. The

British chief steward on *Miss Virginia* was helpful, but not as informative as I'd have liked him to be. "Mrs. Ellis and her party will be lunching on the golf course, sir."

"Which one?" There were a half dozen within ten miles.

"She didn't say, sir. She instructed me to prepare staterooms for Madame de Vargas and yourself. We shall be sailing at eight bells tonight, sir. Twenty hundred hours."

I said we'd be there. But something struck me as a little funny. "Are you telling me those long-haired characters play golf, chief?"

"I should doubt it very much, sir."

"Well, where are they?"

"I believe Miss Valerie is in her stateroom, sir. Mr. McGowan went ashore with Mr. Johnson, just a few minutes ago."

"And Mr. Nichols?"

"I'm not sure, sir."

With Leon de Bas at the hotel, I thought. The steward sounded insolent with disapproval. I dismissed him and hung up, not very satisfied myself. There is a daily dose of decadence available to all of us, if only in the newspapers, yet this one made me bare a tooth. Jacinto Gómez mixed an excellent martini, but the first one of the day tasted a little stale somehow. On the big patio a slightly delayed luncheon of gazpacho, mushroom omelette, and fruit salad was being served. Lita, in beach pajamas, languished at the food. I caught myself eating too much yet not enough. The Gómez couple, it occurred to me, would think about as much of me as I did of the Belgian homosexual. To some extent they might even be justified.

We'd reached the coffee stage when to my vast astonishment the two senior members of the Strawberry Preserves Conspiracy made their appearance, strolling down the beach, passing the pool, and crossing the croquet lawn. When Jacinto moved to intercept them and I waved him back, he stared at me. I didn't blame him in the least. Both boys looked thoroughly disreputable—Mick McGowan in bare, dirty feet and ragged Levi's, Hero Pud in a dashiki like a tent, his Afro hairdo bristling with caked grease. Watching them as they started up the walkway to the patio, Lita raised an eyebrow. "I don't believe it."

"Well, it's true," I said. "You just haven't seen Marcia lately. She's discovered the Now Generation. You don't have to bother with this."

"If you do, I want to," she insisted quietly.

There was no time to make an issue of it since our unexpected visitors had covered half the distance to our table; they were within earshot. I spoke sharply to them. "We're at lunch. If you have something to discuss with me, wait by the pool, please."

"Peace, man," the McGowan lad admonished me. "Like, the old lady said for us to see you. About you-know-what."

"If you mean Mrs. Ellis, I'm quite sure she told you I would meet you on the yacht, sometime this afternoon."

"Right on, man," Hero Pud said. "But it got to be a drag, waiting for you to show."

I studied both of them across my coffee cup. They were so badly out of line that I could only assume they felt ready for a showdown. That meant they'd been well supplied with ammunition by somebody whose identity wasn't particularly hard to guess. "All right," I said. "You fellows goofed last night, missing your plane and getting into trouble with Moroccan currency control. Which means I can't depend on you to do your part. So let's just put you on a plane back to New York tonight, and I'll arrange to have the merchandise delivered to you later. For a fee, of course." This wasn't what they had in mind, but it would serve for openers, I thought.

It didn't. Mick McGowan sneered at me through his Mongolian mustache. "No deal," he told me bluntly.

"No? You have a better idea?"

"Sure, man. Either the old lady takes us all the way, right now. Or she does." He was pointing with his chin at Lita, deep in rapid Spanish conversation with Ana Gómez about the dinner menu of the day. I stared at him, quite genuinely surprised, but he was serious. "She's on a diplomatic passport, isn't she?"

Now we were getting somewhere.

Evidently, there was more to this. Not only was Leon de Bas supplying information to these charming youngsters. He was also using them to demonstrate to me the error of my ways. I had refused to turn off the Rumanian subsidy, or to agree to his preposterous demand that Lita and myself should act as hostages for his security while he attended to his family affairs in Belgium. I had even scorned his kindly offer to "adjust" the Strawberry Preserves Conspiracy. Now he intended to reciprocate, through Lita, if I didn't promptly choose to come around.

Of course he knew that I would never let her take the risk of smuggling drugs. She did indeed carry a diplomatic passport; but although the luggage of a diplomat will normally pass customs unexamined, this is just a courtesy procedure, not to be compared to the inviolable immunity of the so-called diplomatic bag in charge of a courier. And there had been a dozen cases in the past few years of drugs brought in by diplomats from South America. They usually went to jail.

Somehow, Leon de Bas had come to the conclusion that there was a great deal more to my relationship with Lita than the fashionable, jet-set style *affaire de convenance*.

The only thing he could not possibly have realized or understood was that his knowledge forced my hand in a manner quite different from the one he had intended. I put down my coffee cup, touched Lita's arm, and said, in Spanish, "You have canceled dinner for tonight?"

"*Si, claro, mi amor*. We sail for France at eight, *verdad?*"

"Probably not, as it turns out. But do not change your order. We shall see. Meanwhile it might be better if you were to go into the house. Unfortunately there will have to be unpleasantness."

"In that case, I shall certainly stay here." She settled back into her deck chair with the small entr'acte cigar I'd lighted up for her. She watched me closely, half-defiant, half-concerned.

I shrugged and said to our unwelcome visitors: "You fellows seem to think you can get by with this."

They were amused with me. McGowan, grinning, told me: "You're not syndicate. Not even FBI."

"It doesn't matter who or what I am. Whatever in the world makes you believe that it's all right for you to blackmail Mrs. Ellis or this lady? I'm not even talking about whether they'll hold still for it or turn you over to the cops. I want to know what gives you the idea that you can go ahead and do this sort of thing. That there's no ethical or moral problem to it."

"Shit, man, who you sending up?" demanded Hero Pud. "We can do anything to you, no problem."

"Face it, man," McGowan said. "You people are like nowhere." He looked smug and sounded perfectly composed.

I knew exactly what they meant. There were no personalities involved, not from their point of view. They didn't care if Marcia had too much money or if she indulged her special appetites; and they knew practically nothing about Lita, I felt sure—de Bas would have no reason to provide them with a background briefing on her. As for me, they weren't particularly interested, not as long as I was not a gangster or a cop. The only thing that made all three of us abominable to them was the simple fact that we'd been born too soon. This made us war criminals, racial oppressors, and polluters. Nothing was too bad for us, and for a few hundred million like us. Biologically we were people, but most insects took precedence over us.

Some thirty years before, I'd interviewed a lot of German prisoners of war. Most of the Nazi storm troopers were just like that. They saw the population of the world in simple terms. Not altogether by coincidence, most of them were under thirty years of age.

"Let's make quite sure we understand each other," I said patiently. "There are two suitcases on *Miss Virginia*, with fifty kilograms of hashish. You acquired these in a barter deal for your used Volkswagen, or let's say for a thousand dollars, and you want to take them to New York where they'll be worth something like sixty thousand wholesale. I appreciate that you can't see any wrong in taking or in selling drugs. Up to a certain point, that seems to be a matter of opinion. Very well, then, let's suppose I pay you sixty thousand for them here and now, and send you on your way. Will that be satisfactory?"

They were so far ahead of me it was ridiculous. They didn't even laugh at me. "No, man. Like we're in this for fun as much as profit," said McGowan, cheerfully enough.

"You realize I could just grab the stuff and drop you fellows overboard, don't you?"

There now. That was more like it. This was their idea of fun. "You wouldn't, man," said Hero Pud, at last, still choking with hilarity. "You got like ethics, right?"

"I do?"

"Also, we got a friend who knows about your hangup here. He says he can take care of you and her," McGowan said. He glanced at Lita, whose blank stare at him had probably convinced him that she didn't understand.

"Yes, well, your friend is wrong," I said. "Now this is what's going to happen. Mrs. Ellis was advised by me last night to put all four of you ashore and dump your stuff into the harbor. She decided that she'd take you on to France instead. That's up to her, of course, and I shall certainly not interfere with it, but there's a little matter just between ourselves that needs attention. How long has it been since either of you guys was punished for misconduct, such as being rude or nasty in the presence of a lady, using vulgar language, little things like that?''

They looked at me, apparently convinced I'd lost my mind. Perhaps they were correct, for there was certainly no common sense in this. I couldn't possibly get any satisfaction out of it, or hope to make these two young clowns go straight. It seemed to be annoyance that was moving me, which isn't usually my excuse for doing anything at all.

Even Jacinto Gómez, without any English, knew what I was into. He had quietly taken up position a few steps behind our visitors. ''Immobilize the black muchacho,'' I said calmly. ''Do not hurt him.''

''*Si*, señor.'' He got both hands on Hero Pud's right wrist and locked it up between his shoulder blades.

There are some specialists in unarmed combat who can break this hold without losing an arm; and there are people who can instantly quote the cube root of any seven-digit number you might care to mention. Hero Pud stood still, continuing to stare at me in disbelief. His Irish partner, watching me remove the plain black leather belt I didn't need to keep my slacks up, backed away from me. ''You're off your bird, man,'' he informed me, trying hard to make it sound as if he were concerned for me. ''Like, I mean, you're sick.''

I smiled at him, not very pleasantly, and asked him if he'd like to run for it—wasn't he a guerrilla, and weren't they supposed to run? I told him that if he tried putting up a fight he'd probably be damaged, but that the belt wouldn't hurt too much and might do him some good. The best thing he could do, I said, was to bend over and grab ankles, like an English public schoolboy.

He responded with the usual, impractical obscene suggestion. This was stifled by the yelp of pain forced from him by the belt lashing his hips; he snatched at it, but it cut through his fingertips, came back at him, and slashed across his thighs. It could not possibly have harmed him, but it disconcerted him enormously. Most likely nobody had ever castigated him for anything in all his twenty years or so. Wild-eyed, his face working, he rushed me; I just sidestepped him and tripped him; he plopped on his belly on the patio tiles with the breath hissing out of him. I laid the belt on him, not really very hard, administering twenty lashes, systematically, holding him down with a foot between the shoulders when he tried to scuttle off. The first few strokes drew little more than gasps from him, but when his lungs caught up he started keening with exaggerated agony.

"Oh, shut it off," I said, trailing the belt. "That's all there is for you. You ought to thank me, but you probably don't know the words." I turned my back on him and walked over to Hero Pud, still hobbled by Jacinto Gómez. He was watching his companion's problem almost placidly; he had had time to come to terms with the incredible. "Release him," I said evenly, in Spanish.

The Colombian soldier carefully detached his grip and stood aside. Hero Pud looked at me and at the trailing belt, expressionlessly. "Not me, man," he said. "You hassle me, you gonna wish you never tried."

I said he had the same three options—run, or fight, or grab his ankles. He informed me I was full of monkey excrement. He pulled the zipper down on his dashiki, dropped the garment to his feet, stepped out of it, and showed me about one hundred and eighty pounds of fairly well-conditioned meat and bone in jockey shorts. He promised me that if I touched him, baby, he would wipe me out; on this, he recommended that I bet what he defined as my sweet ass. In passing he advised me that I was a verminous white honky racist pig. He spat at me and missed.

"Don't handicap yourself," I said. "I'm not as lily-white as that."

He went for me, not in a silly rush but in a shuffle, stabbing at me with his left, showing me all about his ring experience. I dropped the belt and backed away from him in the direction of the walkway to the pool, and put the afternoon sun in his eyes. I might have kept him busy for a while, with gloves on, in a gym, or bust a knuckle on his jaw right there. But that wasn't the purpose of this exercise.

"Come on, urban guerrilla!"

Stab, stab, blink, blink, stab. I laughed at him and kicked him in the shins, not very hard. His right looped out at me in furious retaliation, brushed past my left ear, and brought his armpit into contact with my shoulder. He went flying through about five yards of empty air and landed on his spine.

Of course the trouble with this unarmed-combat business is that it's terribly hard to control, particularly if you can't take time to practice about twice a week. Hero Pud Johnson was out cold, sprawled on the tiles. I looked at him and walked away from him, picked up my belt and put it on. The Irish kid with the Mongolian mustache had scrabbled to his feet; he flinched at my impatient gesture.

"Do something about your friend."

"Like what?"

"Just wake him up and get him out of here, McGowan," I said testily. "Tell him to take it easy for a week or two. He may have cracked a couple of vertebrae."

She walked into the guestroom I was formally supposed to occupy and watched me check the little Airweight Cobra I'd dug up out of my luggage. "Do you have to carry that?"

"Sometimes."

"You didn't seem to need it with those boys just now."

I gave the door my shoulder. "There's considerable difference between a need and a convenience. I could have used this thing to scare them off."

"But they've gone!"

"Yes, and they won't be back," I said. "And Marcia'll take them off to France at eight o'clock tonight. Maybe she'll even haul them all the way to New York City. If Valerie Gardner plays her cards right."

"Then why . . ." She eyed the gun I'd broken to inspect the barrel and the load. "Are we still sailing with them? Wouldn't it be easier to take a plane?"

"If I were still in business." She caught her breath when she took in what I was saying. "Don't you see, those kids are not the problem. We are."

"But . . ."

"You'd like to know just how Leon de Bas found out about us? So would I. My guess is that he hasn't really, that he's simply playing it by ear. Unfortunately that's as good as if he had the music right before him."

"Steve, it's not! Francisco won't believe him if he has no evidence!"

It wasn't funny, and if it had been I still wouldn't have laughed at her. "You want to take a chance on that?"

This time she saw the point immediately. What was evidence? It seemed unlikely that de Bas had somehow managed to record our private conversations. If he couldn't airmail tapes of them to Bogotá, he could pick up the phone. General Vargas might not take his word for anything, but that was by no means predictable. The caller would not be so unsophisticated as to tell him that his wife was taking me to bed. He'd tell him that I was neglecting my professional affairs for her; that I was brawling over her with younger men. That I was rather obviously in love with her.

Lita de Vargas said: "The gun. You're thinking of Jacinto?"

"And of Ana. Yes, of course I am. And of whoever gets in line behind them."

She confronted me, touching me with her body, looking up at me; the cool green lilac eyes were thoughtful. "How much time?"

"You know as much as I do. How long is the average delay on calls to Bogotá from here? Three hours?"

"Never less than that."

"I can do something to the phone downstairs, but I don't want to. If your husband makes his mind up, he can get through to Jacinto anyway."

A former chief of state can telephone his embassy and have a code message relayed through the police. My watch said 16:45—I should be able to catch Jimmy Dexter in New York before he went to lunch and tell him to put someone else on the Rumanians. I should be making careful, clever plans. We should be packing. Not more than two medium-sized suitcases. One would be better. Lita was asking: "Have you made up yours?"

"Half an hour ago. When Mick McGowan said he had a friend who'd promised to take care of you and me."

"Steve, are you sure he'll try?"

"No, I'm not sure," I said. "Most blackmailers will go away if they're faced down. But then, most blackmailers are amateurs. This man's a pro, and one of his considerations will be that he'll benefit from getting rid of me. Unless he still believes that he can use me. Which I'm very much inclined to doubt."

She backed away, watching me close the gun and pocket it. "Are we definitely breaking with Francisco?"

"Can you see a sensible alternative?"

"No, darling. But it's terribly disheartening."

I stared at her. "It is? You mean you've changed your mind since yesterday?"

"You blockhead," she said coldly in her even-toned, contemptuous, Swiss-finishing-school English. "You insensitive, dull-witted *Indian*. Yesterday I begged you to take me away from him and you refused. You said you were afraid of what his thugs might do to us. Now we don't have a choice, but you can bring yourself to ask me if I've changed my mind. You imbecile." She'd turned her back on me and she was shaking. When I tried to take her in my arms she twisted free and swung on me, a fast right hook. I blocked it, counterpunched instinctively, and barely managed to deflect the blow; it struck her shoulder, spun her half across the room, and spilled her on the bed. She struggled to get up, wincing with pain and failure when her legs wouldn't support her.

"What's the matter?"

"I—you hurt me." She'd come up against the wooden framework of the bed, hitting the back of her right knee, a trivial but momentarily disabling injury. I watched her, standing over her, and she could see the flicker in my eyes, of course. "No," she said anxiously. "No, don't. Please don't."

"Oh yes."

"It will be rape. I don't—don't want you anymore. I'll scream."

"Will you? For Ana and Jacinto? They don't have the word yet. And they've heard you scream before, you know. They don't approve of it, but they expect it."

She spat up at me and missed. I slapped her, grabbed her beach pajamas at the neckline, ripped them to the navel, seized the tattered fabric with both hands, and split it wide apart; the frail white net bikini panties she wore under it disintegrated when I hooked a finger into them. She cursed me, with the supercilious lisp of high Castilian Spanish that can cut like a scalpel, and tried to roll away from me. I stopped her and knelt on the floor between her legs. "It won't be rape," I said.

The sunbeam that awakened me had a low slant, a saffron

iridescence. When I understood the reason for this, every muscle in my body froze in shock. The watch I was still wearing
glittered evilly, unreadably, until I wrenched my arm away
from the reflection. Half past seven, with the minute hand already creeping through the vertical. Beside me, partly covered
by a litter of sheets and pillows, lay the only woman who had
ever overwhelmed me, and who was about to pull my roots out
of the soil in which they'd burrowed for some twenty years
longer than she had lived. Intolerably, she was snoring. Not
unmusically, but the situation raised the hackles on my neck.

"Wake up! We're *asking* for it."

Eyes closed, smiling lazily, she reached for me. I was already off the bed, slamming into my clothes, but something in
that smile and in her semiconscious gesture stabbed me with a
poignant memory. The girl at Texas U. who'd married me,
and borne my son, and lost him, and had left me more than
thirty years ago, had smiled like this and reached for me like
this and quoted Thornton Wilder from her English Lit. *Love
is what makes new life and shelters it.* I shuddered with the
impact of the past, and bit myself back into control. "It's very
late," I said, as evenly as I could manage. "You must shower
quickly and start packing. While I try to get through to New
York."

"*Seguida, mi amor.*" She sat up, looking at me. "New
York? Who is it you are calling there?"

"My boss. He has a right to know as soon as possible."

The Villa Calayán seemed more than usually quiet as I
walked downstairs, but from the living room I could see Ana
Gómez setting out the evening cocktail tapas on the patio. Her
husband did not seem to be around, although he should have
been behind the bar by now. When I approached the phone he
suddenly materialized from the hallway to the servants'
quarters. He stopped short and stared at me as if I were the
last man in the world he had expected to encounter there.

"*Buenas noches*, Señor Harvester."

He always managed to pronounce the H, which was one reason why I doubted that he had no English. Certainly it wasn't my imagination that his stare seemed scornful to the point of insolence. It measured me and lingered well below my waistline where the gun weighed down the right-hand pocket of my sportscoat. Since there was a reasonable possibility that he'd received instructions by now, and that I was actually looking at my executioner, the urge I felt to shoot him on the spot was difficult to overcome. It could be done comparatively easily, right then. He seemed quite confident that he could handle me, that I was unaware of any problem. I would have to kill his wife, as well, of course, and bury both of them. That, also, could be done. The local cleaning girls went home at five.

He wasn't staring at the gun, I realized abruptly. He was disapproving of the zipper in my slacks which in my hasty dressing I'd left down.

I pulled it up, smiled at him bleakly, and reached for the phone. It rang before I got my hands on it. I held down the receiver, gesturing impatiently in the direction of the patio. Jacinto Gómez walked away.

"Digame?"

Marcia Ellis's executive soprano spoke up sharply in my ear. "Steve, is that you? We're *waiting* for you."

". . . We overslept. I'm very sorry, but I don't believe . . ."

Marcia Ellis's executive soprano spoke up sharply in my ear. "Steve, is that you? We're *waiting* for you."

". . . We overslept. I'm very sorry, but I don't believe . . ."

"Did you?"

"Well, you know. The girl is only seventeen, but that's a *passport* figure. Anyway, I told them after breakfast that I wanted them to make other arrangements, and they did, of course. Or someone did. I think it was that swishy Dutchman. He seemed rather *interested* in them, shall we say."

"You mean they've gone? The customs people passed their

luggage?"

"Steve, dear, don't you realize they have to pass it when it's shipped in bond? The local freight agent came by for it at six o'clock."

I made a noise somewhere between a snarl and a groan. I had allowed myself to become so bedeviled by my disaffection for the Strawberries and by a fixed resolve to punish them that easy answers such as this had simply not occurred to me. Leon de Bas had not been quite so muddlebrained. He'd used the issue to put pressure on me, hoping he could still persuade me to cooperate with him; and when that didn't work he'd coolly solved it, partly for his personal convenience, partly to score on me.

Of course he hadn't come up with a genuine solution. Luggage for transshipment in the custody of cargo brokers has to be inspected by some customs officer, somewhere, before its owner can regain possession of it. Probably McGowan and Co. had not been aware of that, and almost certainly their benefactor had not thought it necessary to explain. On the phone Marcia Ellis was still talking to me, scolding me, instructing me to hurry. I paid no attention. Not until she rang the bell a second time.

"*Who* left a message for me, did you say?"

"The Dutchman, dear. He called just a few minutes ago, asking for you. He said to tell you that he is prepared to offer you a better proposition than the one he had for you this morning. He will take it up with you in France."

"He's going there?"

"That's what I understood."

"But not on *Miss Virginia.*"

"No, no. Certainly not."

I said I'd be right over, and hung up, and strode out on the patio. The Gómez couple, stolidly immaculate in servants' livery, offered their usual, impassive Mayan scowls. "*Qué pasa?*

We shall not be dining here tonight. You were informed of this by Doña Isabella."

"*Sí, señor.*"

"Well, then, what are you doing here?"

"We have received no orders canceling your cocktail hour, señor."

"You have them now," I said. "Also, you will close up this house tomorrow morning. In the afternoon, you'll fly to Nice —there is a KLM plane out of Málaga at three o'clock. You will be met by someone sent by Mrs. Ellis's *jefe de casa.*"

They didn't seem to hear me for what must have been at least ten seconds. That is a considerable length of time for people to look straight into each other's eyes. In theirs, the ancient, feral malice of the jungle Indian smoldered unmistakably. I wondered what they saw in mine; perhaps it was the careful scrutiny my grandmother in Santa Fé used to bestow on her selection from the pen when it came time to put up a supply of ham and bacon for the winter.

Ana Gómez never blinked. It was Jacinto who, at last, jerked back his shoulders and perfunctorily clicked his heels.

ANTIBES, WEDNESDAY, JULY 21.

As I'd suspected, the Rumanian delegation was clandestine and provincial: one man came from Jassy, one from Braila, both of these being substantial market towns located near the Russian border, if you're going to define the Ukraine as Russian which, of course, it isn't. They were very carefully not introduced to me when Yuri Franklin brought me in; their geographical constituencies happened to leak out during the meeting. Both looked to be reasonably solid people, as Rumanians go, although they would be Party members or they couldn't have been there at all.

The younger of the two could speak a little French. He was the short-haired, bullnecked one who actually wore a shirt and tie with his black homespun suit. He also was the one who kept haranguing me on how much better off every peasant in Rumania is these days. His partner had magnificent white sideburns with his walrus mustache, and appeared content to offer me a patriarchal smile of dubious approval. Yuri had already told me that they'd visited the alternate pretender, Michael, in his villa behind Cannes, the day before. Apparently they'd come away unsatisfied, or open to a better deal.

"You are a journalist, monsieur?"

"That's right."

"But you have money from your government in Washington for us?"

"No. I have money for His Majesty, subject to certain understandings. I can make no statement about where this money comes from."

We had gathered in the library of the Château Lucardi, which is Marcia Ellis's seventeenth-century estate, built in a twenty-acre park of deodars in 1934. Behind the genuine Louis XIV desk sat Carol Rudolph Ferdinand von Hohenzollern-Sigmaringen, *soi-disant*, looking for all the world as though he were a ruling monarch granting inconvenient audience to commoners. His beautifully tailored dinner jacket almost but not quite concealed the scarlet ribbon that diagonally spanned his bosom, probably the grand cordon of something founded by his great-grandfather twice removed. At his left elbow stood Prince Otto Sturza, very straight and very old, his bitter stare focused somewhere over our heads on something merely sixty years or so into the past. On one of the two rollback sofas, Yuri Franklin posed as Madame Récamier, demurely costumed in high-necked, long-skirted white chiffon; behind her I leaned on the Gobelin-draped wall facing the delegation seated on the second sofa.

"What we wish to know is how much further support Washington will give us."

"In what circumstances?"

". . . When we are able to recall His Majesty."

My bullnecked friend had answered that one pretty glibly, but not really fast enough. Even Prince Sturza noticed, and brought down the ancient shotgun muzzles of his stare on him. Carol himself turned on his thin-lipped British movie actor sneer but made no comment. It was Yuri who demanded casually: "When will you be ready to do that?"

"As soon as we are satisfied of adequate support, madame."

What they were trying to put over, on each other and on

me, was that they could lay on an instant coup d'état. The funny part of it was that they actually could, because the average Rumanian hates Mother Russia even more intensely than do most Hungarians, Poles, or Czechs, and beyond that remains emotionally and traditionally hidebound to the monarchy. The problem was, of course, that any such shenanigans would only last about three days.

But not if Moscow were to be kept busy otherwise. Even the lobster-red Ceauşescu government was diligently cultivating both Peking and Washington with some such thought in mind.

These boys, on both sides of the desk, were only interested in their pocketbooks for now, which was exactly why they interested Jimmy Dexter, in New York, who didn't have much use for patriots. "There will be money," I said carefully. "Sufficient money for our common purposes. The source of it is not available for identification or discussion. It will be supplied in Switzerland or in West Germany. Our auditors are to review your propositions and to countersign the checks. Emergency funds, up to a negotiated figure, will be at His Majesty's immediate disposal without prior auditing."

The delegation scowled at me. Carol allowed me a raised eyebrow. Sturza bristled. "You presume too much, sir," he said coldly.

"If I do, Your Highness, there's a simple reason for it."

"Be so good as to explain."

"Experience, Your Highness. Quite a great deal of experience."

Yuri laughed her tinkly little geisha laugh. It admirably served to clear the atmosphere. Her royal paramour managed a lofty smile. The bullnecked lad from Jassy chuckled; snowy muttonchops from Braila guffawed, although I was reasonably sure that he had no idea what we were into. Sturza pursed his thin, gray lips at me. "Perhaps your principals would rather have us making a *démarche* to the Chinese," he offered dryly in his faultless diplomatic French.

"My principals would have no reason to prefer that possibility," I said. "Or to object to it."

Five thousand Swiss francs comes to about sixteen hundred dollars, hardly an unreasonable monthly fee for services performed in violation of high confidence. But it was all she'd asked for, and I hadn't really decided yet to pay it to her. Not because I didn't trust her—there is no such animal as a dependable informer—trust is not an element of the transaction. What had put me off was something very nearly undefinable. The closest I could come to it was that I didn't understand her, that she didn't seem entirely human. This was not at all concerned with her being half-Japanese, or with her sexual philosophy: I'd dealt with ladies on the loose before, and with Eurasians. But if someone had come along and seriously suggested that Miss Yuri Franklin had been landed by a spaceship, I'd have found myself considering the possibility.

The fact remained that I would have to pay her. She was obviously in a position to assist me or to bother me. So far, she'd done almost too good a job of both.

This had been brought out pretty clearly on the trip on *Miss Virginia* during the past two days.

On Monday night, at cocktails, she had managed beautifully to relieve the shock effect of my appearance on the scene. Prince Sturza, bowing over Marcia's hand, froze into granite. Carol III, preoccupied with Lita, who'd preceded me on deck by a few minutes, stared at me in disbelief when I walked up. ". . . Ah, er, Harvester! An unexpected pleasure."

"Not to me, Your Majesty."

"Indeed?" My tone had left him in no doubt of what I meant, but he could hardly say so. "Are We to understand that you are traveling with us?"

Since at that very moment *Miss Virginia* had cleared the

Puerto Banus breakwater and entered the Mediterranean, I saw no point in answering his question. "There is work to do, Your Majesty."

"Oh, certainly. Of course."

"The question, Monsieur Harvester," said Sturza icily, "is how you managed to intrude like this."

"I wonder just how much respect Your Highness would have had for me if I had failed to do my job," I said.

Miss Yuri Franklin, sweetly treacherous, inquired: "You mean you *knew*? About the delegation? And that we were going to stand you up until we had found out what they could do for us?"

Sturza ignored her. Carol smiled at her, thinly. I merely shrugged and said: "That is my job, mademoiselle," and the arrival of the British steward with his trayload of champagne shifted the conversation into formal social channels at this point. Dinner turned into something even less of a convivial affair. Marcia Ellis seemed determined, after all, to add another specimen of royalty to her collection—at a guess, the twentieth or twenty-first. Perhaps by way of retaliation, Yuri openly played up to me. Across the wardroom table, Lita watched and sulked, Prince Sturza glowered. Coffee and liqueurs on deck made no improvement—not even an ocean like perfumed black taffetas shimmering under a lemon crescent of a moon seemed capable of bringing any sort of harmony. His Majesty chose to neglect his hostess and to concentrate on Lita, who perversely managed to encourage Marcia to compete for her. This monkey foolishness had lasted half an hour when the chief steward spoke into my ear. There was a phone call for me in the radio shack.

The duty operator proved to be a Pakistani youngster, smartly uniformed and turbaned. "Very sorry to disturb you, sah. The gentleman insisted that he speak with you himself."

"What gentleman?"

"A foreign gentleman, sah. He refused to give his name. The call was placed through Radio Maritime Toulon."

The phone stood on the message desk. I picked it up, watched him flick a switch, and spoke my name. Leon de Bas's epicene inflections came over the carrier wave, perfectly preserved. "Good evening, my dear fellow. Has the captain mentioned your arrival time in Cannes?"

"It'll be shortly after breakfast, day after tomorrow."

"Splendid! Take a walk on the Croisette that morning, will you? Try between eleven and eleven-thirty."

"What's the point, de Bas? There's nothing I can do for you."

He chuckled. "But there is, my boy. I'm sure of it. You see, I haven't been completely frank with you."

"Oh, haven't you?"

"We shall make progress if we treat each other with respect and confidence." He actually sounded persuasive. "Please believe me. There are reasons. Brussels will agree, you'll see."

I said that he'd be better off talking to Brussels, not to me. The carrier wave hissed empty. After a few seconds the French operator in Toulon came on and told me that the caller had hung up.

Outside the radio shack, on the boat deck, Yuri Franklin leaned against the rail and into *Miss Virginia*'s twenty-five knot breeze that made a body paint job of her coral shantung gown. "You've heard from your organization in New York, Steve Harvester?"

"About your salary? Not yet. But their approval is a matter of formality. I'll need the name of your Swiss bank."

She fingered the lapels of my white dinner jacket and looked up into my eyes. "Also the number," she said, coolly businesslike, "of my account. It's in my stateroom. And I have the only key to that."

I put an arm around her waist. She promptly settled into it

and stood on tiptoes, bending over backward. "You've forgotten something, haven't you, my child," I said.

Her laughter rang a challenge with its little silver bell. "Too old for me, are you?"

"Of course I am. I'm just a dirty, lecherous, violent old man."

"But I *like* dirty, lecherous, violent old men. Here, let me show you." She was laughing silently by then, an open-mouthed, sharp-toothed, lubricious laugh that went a little cold when she glanced past me. I was not especially surprised. The breeze had for some time carried the pungency of black Colombian cigarette tobacco to my nose.

Lita de Vargas stood beside the radio shack in a careless, hipshot pose, a fashion model waiting for the camera. "Go right ahead, Miss Franklin," she said casually. "Show him. He's quite easy to convince."

"He must be," Yuri said. She slipped out of my arm and snapped her compact mirror open, stepping back into a light beam from the bridge to check her makeup. Both her tone and action were as mild as tiger's milk. "Excuse me, please, Señora Vargas. It's my fault, of course, but I just didn't *realize* we were competing." She conferred a brilliantly dishonest smile on us and strolled off gracefully to the main deck companionway.

Lita said calmly: "Do you have to humor scum like that?"

"Sometimes," I said. "Not often. Usually they're not very pretty, and they're only interested in the money, or in politics. Sometimes they have a score to settle, with my help. It's what I do. You've known that for two years."

"Give me a cigarette, please." The green lilac eyes flashed up at me under their lashes. ". . . You really look on it as just another job?"

"Of course."

"You're not involved at all? You don't *believe* in it?"

"Oh, yes. Pragmatically speaking, I believe in it. You've got to bear in mind that Moscow actually wants to take over the world and paint it red. So does Peking, a slightly deeper shade, but they don't seem to be as far along with it just yet. The problem seems to be that almost nobody is coping with these bandits. Not effectively."

"Are you?"

"I think we are. Within our limitations, we do better on a fifty-million dollar budget than the CIA and the Department of Defense on eighty billion. You can't stop aggression or prevent a war by sending half a million soldiers into sinkholes like Korea or Vietnam. Five thousand superbombs in silos and on submarines can't stop it. Or a hundred thousand spies and counterspies. The other side can always match those chips and raise you, cheaply, and they have another big advantage over you—you don't particularly want to play this game. *They* do. You don't want to take over. They do. And they'll try, unless they're not quite certain of themselves and of each other. That's what interests us. Insecurity like that can be created, and it can be bought. Comparatively inexpensively. We've bought it and created it for twenty years."

"Oh, was that what you were creating just now?" Lita said maliciously. "Well, I didn't like it, and I'll scratch that trollop's eyes out if she makes another pass at you."

"You'd better not. I'm paying for them."

"Shall I take Carol away from her? My eyes are just as good as hers and they don't slant."

"Why borrow trouble? You don't need the money. This girl does, or seems to think she does," I said, mock-reasonably. "Now here's something else. Our Belgian friend was on the blower. He insists on seeing me again."

"In France? Isn't that rather dangerous for him?"

"It's NATO territory. But the Reds are nicely organized in there. He can get in and he can get protection, under cover."

". . . What does he *want?*"

"I've told you that. He wants to go to Belgium. I can probably arrange it, but not on his terms—they're not exactly realistic. Which disturbs me, since he should know better. On the
other hand, it follows that he hasn't tattled on us to your husband, yet. Apparently he means to keep a stick behind the
door. I have in mind getting my hands on it and beating out
his brains with it."

She crushed her cigarette against a lifeboat stanchion, dropping the dead stub over the rail. For a long moment she
seemed to be listening intently to the hiss of wake and bow
wave, and to *Miss Virginia*'s subdued Diesel drone.

"Steve, darling . . ."

"Hm?"

"Don't bother. It is probably unnecessary."

"Why do you say that?"

"I'm four days overdue this month. And this is the first boat
trip that my stomach hasn't liked."

The delegation was becoming restive, listening to Sturza's
argument with me. Since we were speaking French, they had at
least some notion of the subject, but the issue thoroughly elud-
ed them. I had announced that there was money on hand to fi-
nance Carol's restoration. It was inconvenient that I wanted an
accountant in West Germany to check the bills, but they felt
pretty confident that they could diddle him. Sturza might have
mistakenly agreed with them, if he had thought about it. His
objection was that one does not impose a bookkeeper on
royalty.

We had been wrangling over this and about similar antique
delusions on his part since early morning of the day before on
the high seas.

I'd come across the three of them beside the tiny swimming
pool on *Miss Virginia*'s stern: Yuri taking the sun, Carol
drinking his breakfast, while the elderly retainer stood behind

their deck chairs, jauntily attired in flannel slacks, blazer, and yachting cap. Marcia Ellis never put in an appearance before lunchtime. Lita had refused me entrance to the bath we shared. I'd borrowed the first mate's electric razor and decided on a dip. There wasn't any action, sensible or otherwise, that I could take until we docked in France six hundred miles ahead.

Sturza stared through me, but his charges greeted me almost too cordially. "Ah, Harvester. *Good* morning. Won't you join us?"

"With Your Majesty's permission. And Miss Franklin's."

Yuri's grin seemed almost out of character. "When does the interview begin?" she asked.

"The interview?"

"Your *Esquire* magazine story about Carol," she reminded me.

"Oh, that's already set in type. Somebody on their staff wrote it three weeks ago, under my byline. All we need is a few pictures at this point. We can take care of those in Cannes."

The man who looked like Cary Grant shook a few capsules of B-complex vitamin from their container, washed them down with half a tumbler load of vodka, and sat back to watch me jump into the pool and cross it in two strokes. When I popped up he said, goodhumoredly enough: "We trust your story will refrain from pointing out that in this century Rumania has been prevailed on twice into declaring war on Russia. With unfortunate results."

"But not by us, Your Majesty," I said. "By Germany, both times. America doesn't want anybody to make war on anybody else. And where the Soviets are concerned, we're only interested in preventing them from feeling capable of finishing what they might start."

"I am inclined," said Sturza, testily, "to doubt that when we are restored to Bucarest we shall be able to depend upon continuing American support. Or, for that matter, that what your organization offers to provide us in financial assistance at this time will serve to compensate the hazards you require us to accept."

I'd have enjoyed explaining to him that we didn't really expect him to get into trouble with the Russians, and that we weren't actually interested in restoring Carol—only in the plausibility of such a restoration at the proper, awkward time. Instead, I said: "Your Highness, if I may speak frankly, that is not the point."

"Indeed? Perhaps you will enlighten me, sir."

"As you wish. The issue, as we see it, seems quite simple. In due course, His Majesty proposes to return to Bucarest. Our offer is to supply funds as well as technical advice. The purpose would be to coordinate his followers, and to assist them in convincing others. And, of course, to make a contribution to the maintenance of his establishment in exile."

Carol poured himself a refill from the almost-empty vodka bottle. "Well, you asked for frankness, my dear Sturza," he said jovially. "There you have it."

"Technical advice!" The elderly aristocrat bared half the dentures under his gray cavalry mustache. "A nice name for coercion. They will tell us what to do, Your Majesty."

He was exactly right, of course. I shrugged and climbed out of the pool. Yuri was offering me coffee and a solemn little wink. Her royal paramour seemed to be quietly amused. "They're paying for the privilege," he said. "But possibly not quite enough."

I liked him better then, because it meant he had decided to play ball. He wasn't in a bargaining position, and he knew it— even Sturza knew it—all they could expect of me was courteous pretense, perhaps a few more small concessions, and a patient ear for what they thought of as their problems. Even that much I begrudged them. It seemed altogether likely that I wouldn't be around to follow through.

Lita was playing deck tennis with the chief engineer when I went up to dress for lunch, and she was beating him; her color had returned, and she was moving well, not sparing herself making the tricky catches, snapping back the ring with body-English and considerable drive. She was most certainly not seasick. That left very little doubt about the nature of her earlier indisposition. I stood by to watch her while my mind— what there was left of it—reviewed once more the options that were open to us.

These had occupied my past three sleepless nights.

Even without the crippling handicaps of pregnancy and childbirth, our survival chances were so slight they hardly merited consideration. Criminals in hiding have a relatively easy time of it, because policemen are not very highly motivated as a rule. Even the specialists in fugitive pursuit at Interpol and Scotland Yard and in the FBI carry such heavy workloads and are normally so much inclined to civil service habit patterns that it's fairly simple to avoid them—all it really takes is sensible discretion and an adequate supply of untraceable money. But the half-dozen "detective agencies" that make a business of finding people who have bothered other people are as highly motivated as their fee and their expense allowance. They will trace a man whose death certificate was filed six weeks ago in Denver, Colorado, where he had a fatal traffic accident, and they'll catch up with him in some unlikely spot such as Uganda or Tasmania, no problem. Then they'll serve the legal papers on him, or they'll break his arms and legs, or they'll set up a traffic accident for keeps.

There's such a thing as thinking positively, isn't there, about such matters. There I was, with more than thirty years' experience in the departments of survival and of dirty tricks. Riding a million-dollar yacht bound for the French Riviera, in the company of the one woman in the world who really meant something to me and who seemed likely to be carrying my child. Yet there occurred to me only two possible devices that might turn off our conversion into buzzard meat within the next few months.

The obvious one was to kill the general myself, without compunction and without delay. It could be done, even without Lita's approval or her knowledge. Vargas would receive me if I took a plane to Bogotá and conned him on the phone. A concentrated, lethal form of insulin can be administered in food or drink, or by a power hypodermic that looks like a cigarette case and will penetrate through cloth and skin, and leave no mark.

I'd thought about that one a lot, and lost a pint of icy sweat every time. It would be physically easy, and it would be almost safe. But it would take a special kind of ruthlessness I might not have acquired in thirty years.

The second choice was nearly equally self-evident to me.

Surprisingly enough, it's possible to hide behind the Iron Curtain. This takes nerve, but not as much as might seem indicated, and it takes forged documents, available in Vienna as a matter of routine and at a reasonable price. There are as many as a hundred thousand Spanish-speaking exiles spread all over Eastern Europe, many of them in their seventies and eighties, most of them politically splintered into scores of little groups. The best three countries would be Hungary and Yugoslavia and, of course, Rumania, but to fugitives they all present one notable advantage. An investigator on a manhunt from the western world will find it very difficult to operate in them.

I'd gray my hair, and put on twenty years, and settle with my newly widowed daughter and my grandchild in a cottage on Lake Balaton. The money would be her late husband's. He was French. He'd had a heart attack. They'd have no reason to check any of that out in Hungary.

It could be done. It was good thinking. But it probably would not be good enough.

The delegation had lost patience with the bullnecked man from Jassy interrupting us, addressing Sturza in Rumanian, making a lengthy speech that was presumably not for my ears. I knew what he was talking about anyway; the language is sufficiently close to French, and since he was a politician there was only one thing he could possibly be interested in.

He'd get his hands on some of it, but not as much as he was after. Also, he'd find out a little later that we were expecting value and performance for it, and that failure to deliver same would have unwelcome consequences.

My attention wandered back once more, this time to the events of that same Wednesday morning. *Miss Virginia* had docked in the big yacht harbor of Cannes at ten A.M. I had been up since eight, pacing the decks, squinting into the sunrise from the bridge, drinking too many cups of coffee. Lita's morning sickness had arrived on schedule, and she'd chased me out again as soon as the first symptoms made themselves evident. By ten o'clock she managed to sit up, push the contents of her breakfast tray around, and look at me, half-rueful, half-defiant. ". . . Want me to see a doctor?"

"Yes, of course. Today, if possible. It's probably too early for a test, but he can give you medicine to settle your digestion. If there's one thing we don't need, it's Ana Gómez catching on."

"We'd better stay here on this boat then," she said reasonably. "Not at the château. I'll speak to Marcia about it."

"No," I said. "I will. She'd ask you to explain. But you will have to phone Jacinto or he might start wondering. This morning, while I pay a visit to our Belgian friend."

"You're meeting him? Alone?" She saw me smile, but she was fretful. "Will there be trouble?"

"If he asks for it."

"Oh *damn*! This *frightful* job of yours. What must I do to make you give it up?" She bit into a piece of toast, viciously, gagging on it, forcing it down. "Shall I ask the doctor for a D and C? Would you like that?"

"No. I won't say I haven't thought about it. It would be a possible solution. But it isn't what I want."

She burst into tears. I moved the tray, sat down on the bed, and took the necessary time to reassure her that I wasn't really a callous, evil-minded, savage Indian. Then it was already past eleven and I had to talk myself into what needed to be done.

The Boulevard de la Croisette runs down the beach from the casino to the harbor. It is not quite as impressive as it used to be, and in July and August it acquires the raffish aspect of too many other major tourist traps. The walk I had been asked to take amounted to a mile of wading through humanity on holiday. I'd managed less than half of it when Yuri Franklin pulled my sleeve.

She had a table by herself at a small sidewalk café opposite the Carlton; she was wearing the same starched white linen mini caftan she had used on me last week in Tangier at the Rif Hotel. "Looking for me, Steve Harvester?"

I took the vacant chair, sat back in it, and stared at her. Coincidences happen and this just might be one. "Aren't you supposed to move to the château?"

"Aren't you?"

I said I hadn't made my mind up, but that I would see the delegation there at four. The situation was a little difficult. I'd seen Carol and Sturza leave the yacht with Marcia in her limousine right after breakfast. Yuri Franklin grinned her oddly boyish little grin. "I didn't finish packing," she said calmly.

"Any special reason?"

"Well, you know. It doesn't always pay to be too punctual. They'll pick me up for lunch; I may have finished then or I may not."

"Yes, that makes sense."

"You're meeting someone, right?"

I wanted her to be sharp but not necessarily that sharp. "Maybe I am," I said. "But certainly not here."

A busy waiter put a Dubonnet before me that I hadn't ordered. It seemed easier to pay him for it than to make him take it back. The brief delay was just enough to cause the sort of difficulty I was trying to avoid. You don't, if you can help it, let an agent in your pay make eyeball contact with another, and much less with prospects or with messengers from prospects.

In this case the messenger turned out to be a peddler, one of those Algerian part-clowns, part-thieves who roam all over Europe with a shoulder load of sleazy Oriental rugs and hassock covers. He'd been working on some of the nearby tourist tables with a soft-sell pitch that didn't seem to be getting him anywhere. I was already on my feet when he latched on to Yuri, and to me. *"Pouf-pouf, m'si-dame? Pouf-pouf, joli tapis?"*

She smiled for him and shook her head. I waved him off, impatiently, dim-wittedly, and he insisted upon handing me his card. This had been printed with a stencil set, and badly smudged, but it looked new. It called him Achmed Saladin, Import-Export, supplying his address as Rue Marat 121, Bruxelles. Since it seemed most unlikely that he lived in Brussels, or that he would want me to know all about it, or that any street in Belgium would be named after a personage of the French revolution, it was fairly clear what he might have in mind.

"He knows you, doesn't he," said Yuri, and she wasn't smiling anymore. I shrugged, but she stayed with it. "Are you going somewhere?"

"Why?"

"Oh, I just wondered if it's something, you know, dangerous?"

That made two women in one morning worrying about me.

"Yes, it is," I said. "It means I'll have to cross this boulevard. Goodbye, Miss Franklin. See you at the meeting. Don't forget to let me have the number and the name of your Swiss bank account."

The cab driver admitted that there was a Rue Marat in Cannes. This proved to be a long, dull street of tenements, small shops, and bars. One-twenty-one was in the middle of the second block. I had been reasonably sure that it would be a vacant lot, and so it was—rather a tidy one, the rubble cleared away, the weeds kept down, a realtor's For Sale sign firmly staked. Apparently I was expected to play treasure hunt in there. I shrugged and went along with it, leaving the taximeter ticking on the street behind me. But it became obvious soon enough that nothing more significant awaited me than the realtor's phone number and a dead and decomposing cat.

By then I'd crossed the lot and reached the alley bordering it—nothing special, just a strip of cobblestone between adjoining buildings, most of them blank-walled, no garbage cans in sight. From the next cross street a big dump truck was reversing very slowly into it. The driver's helper saw me, raised an arm, and waved me back; the truck was fifty yards away, filling the alley like a bullet fills the barrel of a gun.

It was a setup, calculated carefully to put me on the hook. They had in mind for me not to react like normal people. If the man had beckoned to me, I'd most probably have walked away from him, but as it was he caused me to suspect that there was something in the alley I wasn't supposed to see. The memory of Wahlstrom's problem in Tangier failed to discourage me. A heavy truck in low reverse can be outrun by anyone on wooden legs.

There were three back doors and a few barred windows within easy distance. I had time to try them all, and all of them were locked, the windows painted black. This little expedition put me where they wanted me, about five yards from the flat backside of the moving dump truck and fifteen or so into the alley, and of course they had a second truck behind me at that point, boxing me in, the noise of its approach muffled by the exhaust roar of the first. I didn't bother wasting any breath on criticizing my poor judgment or their doubtful ancestry. The options were a dive between the wheels or kicking in the nearest door.

I kicked and had the silly, slapstick movie-style experience of meeting no resistance with my heel and landing on my spine, on what felt like a dusty wooden floor. Before the door slammed shut on total darkness there was an unsettling glimpse of a half a dozen nude male corpses that seemed to be hanging about the premises. I rolled away from them and got my feet back under me, my body in a crouch, unhappy with myself about it all, and at that point a narrow light beam stabbed at me. It pinned me down, but it had swept across the funeral exhibit. This turned out to be a small collection of wax dummies. I was in the storeroom of a tailor shop.

Behind the light, Leon de Bas said cheerfully: "You'll pardon these precautions, 'Arvestair. I have not yet succeeded in developing my confidence in you."

"Makes two of us," I said. "You can stop worrying already. I'm alone."

"The proof of that is that you are alive." A fluorescent ceiling fixture flickered on. The storeroom was a good deal larger than I'd estimated. Most of it was empty space and all the way across this, at least thirty feet away, de Bas lounged in a swivel chair behind the desk reflector lamp that had supplied the beam. He clicked it off and watched me dust my pants. "I am not very pleased with you, my dear boy."

"Suit yourself."

"Unfortunately I cannot, since time will not permit."

I stared at him and at the man who stood between us to one side and facing me, a young French underworld type with a forty-dollar hairstyle and about five hundred dollars' worth of flashy wardrobe on his back that almost made me overlook the switchblade he was using to clean out his nails. "On the phone the other night you mentioned something about progress. Is this it?"

"I shall explain," de Bas said coldly. "Two things have occurred. The Dancing Dog schedule has been advanced. Also, my personal affairs in Belgium have become more urgent."

"Care to tell me what they are?"

"I do not. You are not concerned with them." The swivel chair groaned in alarm when he sat forward in it. "What you are to understand is that we have no time. Not to complete arrangements for protection of my personal security."

"You mean you'll skip the hostage bit," I said.

His scowl would have impressed me if my own exasperation with him had been any less. "My circumstances are compelling me to trust you, 'Arvestair."

"With what?"

"You will communicate with Brussels. You'll inform them that the Dancing Dog conduit will be opened tomorrow. It will carry a supply of a new rabies virus, a mutation that will spread by air, like influenza."

"Talk to them yourself, man," I said scornfully.

He didn't seem to hear me. "Tell them that I will reveal to you, tonight, the mechanism of the conduit and its operators. They will have twelve hours to control my information."

"So?"

"If it should prove correct, they will admit me into Belgium for two weeks without molesting me. Tomorrow night."

"I just don't know, de Bas," I said. "Why should I bother making like your messenger boy? What's in this for me?"

He took a little time with that and seemed to weigh his words. ". . . Very well. I shall permit you to complete your business with these preposterous Rumanians."

"You will?"

"Spare me your childish mockery, please, my dear fellow.

You came here because you realize I am in a position to request a favor of you. It will be unfortunate, to say the least, if you refuse me." As usual he managed to sound slimily insinuating. "For Señora Vargas. Probably for you as well."

At least we understood each other at this point. He still intended to keep hostages. Not in Morocco, in his mountain cabin, but right here in France, or anywhere we chose to go in the next fourteen days. "You really need this bodyguard of yours," I said. "Suppose I have a message for you later on, will you be here all night?"

"No, no, my boy." He almost laughed at me out loud before he pointed at the French gorilla with the knife. "You are to meet Jean-Claude tonight at seven-thirty. On the boardwalk at Juan-les-Pins."

The delegation shook my hand in farewell with much vigor and solemnity. The patriarch from Braila who could speak no French allowed my cheeks the prickly benefit of his white sideburns. "A*may*rica—okay!"

"Yes, sir."

"Roosevelt—you—okay!"

"Uh, thank you, sir."

Nobody laughed at me, not even Yuri. Sturza's shotgun-muzzle eyes stared out into the park of the Château Lucardi. Carol, standing behind Marcia Ellis's Louis XIV desk, returned the delegation's bow and watched its ceremonious, backside-first withdrawal from the room. He casually glanced at me after the door had closed and poured himself a drink that finished his third vodka bottle of the day, according to my estimate. "It seems to us you satisfied them," he admitted, more or less reluctantly.

"Let's hope that they will satisfy Your Majesty," I said, and tactfully omitted mentioning that Jimmy Dexter in New York would also have to be.

I'd reached him after lunch, which was about nine-thirty in the morning New York time, and he had listened without comment while I talked about Leon de Bas in terms and phrases of a business deal between television packagers. "You want me to approach the European network people with it?"

He said no, he didn't think so. He would call them and find out if they were interested in the story line. If so, they could get back to me without delay, and they could quote their own priorities—he meant the level of command and telephone security they might assign to it. I told him that in my opinion they'd refuse to buy the program, but that they might like to cast the actor in a different production. He agreed with me and said he'd check out the idea with a few sponsors stateside, and he wanted me to keep in touch.

The Brussels operator came in on the line within ten minutes, asking for me. She put on a voice I'd heard before, a heavy bass with gravel on its bottom, unmistakable as black American. Three years ago, in Wiesbaden, West Germany, that voice in no uncertain terms had told me to get out of town. Its owner bore a pair of colonel's eagles on the shoulders of a body like a tank. "You know me, fella?"

"Yes, sir, I believe I do."

"Some cop in Tangier spoke to me about you. Just what did Sven Wahlstrom get into with you at three A.M. last Saturday?"

"I have no way of knowing, Colonel," I said patiently. "He seemed to think I work for Washington. The man he was involved with is in Cannes right now. You want him?"

"You're damn fucking right I want him. I'll send down a couple of my boys on the next plane."

"You understand he wants to make a deal, sir, don't you?"

"Sure I understand. No deals, fella. We get our hands on him, we drop him down where he belongs and pull the chain."

He blew disgust into the phone, explosively. "Rabies, for

God's sake! The cat's out of his fucking mind!"

I said: "He may be all of that, Colonel, but just the same, I never did care for that code name, Dancing Dog. Somebody has a nasty sense of humor, and it isn't our fat Belgian friend."

"Listen, the Russkies just don't operate that way." He suddenly sounded almost goodnatured, lecturing to me. "They'd like to put us down, all right, if they could do it without getting clobbered while they were about it. But they're gunners, rocketeers—it's got to be with a big bang, you know? Of course they've got B.W. *capacity*. Hell, any two-bit country with a medical school can wipe out the human race."

"What bothers me is that our friend says he will trust us," I said carefully.

"So he'll find out how wrong he was." The chuckle that arrived over the line would have collapsed my liver, if I'd been de Bas. "Put him on ice for me, please, will ya, fella? Until we can get there."

"Put the cops on him, you mean?"

"Sure, why not? He's a fruit. Charge him with groping you. They'll hold him on that overnight."

"I'll see what can be done," I said. "What are those urgent personal affairs of his in Belgium, colonel, do you know?"

"Yeah, I know all about 'em. It's his mother."

"What?"

"Would you believe it?" Once more that ferocious chuckle. "She's eighty-two, and she's got cancer of the uterus. He wants to see her. Grabs you, doesn't it?"

When I rejoined Marcia Ellis on the terrace overlooking the Château Lucardi's rose garden she raised an eyebrow at me. "Steve, dear, you seem positively *saturnine*. What's going wrong, or can you tell?"

"Business problems. Nothing I can't handle."

She knew just enough to keep from offering me money. "It's about that swishy Dutchman, isn't it? What are you doing to him?"

"Actually, I'm not interested in him."

"But you've seen him, haven't you," she shrewdly diagnosed. "And he insists on doing business with you?"

I shrugged and said that might be so. "The trouble is, he
doesn't seem to have the merchandise."

"Why do you bother with him, then?" She rose, took my
arm, and walked away with me into the garden. "Why do you
and Lita want to stay on *Miss Virginia*? You'd be much more
comfortable here."

"And much less private."

"Steve dear, you're not being altogether frank with me, are
you. You two don't *need* that sort of privacy. *Everybody* knows
about you."

"I hope not."

"Of course they do. Two years ago there was some tittle-tat-
tle, for a while, but everybody *understood*. About her husband
being sensible and everything. Even the servants . . ."

"What about them?"

"Why, they *like* you, Geoffrey tells me. They *approve*. Now
that's unusual, you know."

I tried to think of Ana and Jacinto Gómez liking me. It
didn't seem impossible. There are a lot of people who efficiently mask their feelings. "As it happens, Marcia," I said slowly,
"we can't stay. We'd love to, you know that, but there are
reasons. I intend to sew up the Rumanians this afternoon, as
much as possible. Tonight or early in the morning we'll be
going back to Spain."

It didn't seem a very good idea to tell her why. She might
not have believed me, in which case I couldn't have relied on
her discretion; or, believing me, she might have worried, one
way or another, and a wealthy woman with a worry on her
mind can buy a lot of trouble with the best intentions in the
world. Leon de Bas had to be put away, of course. If Section
Six, miraculously, had agreed to work with him, I might have
reconsidered, but under the circumstances it was imbecile to

turn him over to them or to let him stay alive.

I wondered why he failed to realize this. The black NATO colonel had advanced an explanation, but I didn't think the man was mad. He actually seemed to be convinced somehow that what he had was good enough. He seemed to feel he could protect himself.

Maybe he could, but I was going to find out.

There is, of course, a basic similarity between the boardwalk at Juan-les-Pins and those at Brighton, Coney Island, and Atlantic City. But the difference in setting and in atmosphere amounts to a considerable contrast. Here there is no tide or surf, no summer breeze. The sallow ribbon of the beach is packed from dawn to midnight. Cactus, palms, and pine trees line the narrow promenade, haphazardly. The cheap hotels and boardinghouses, bar-cafés and vending stalls crowd in on every square inch available. At dusk, the very moment when the photochemical detergent action of the sun diminishes below a certain point, arrives the curious phenomenon of the big stench that seems to rise up instantly from land and sea, a rotten-fish scent that is formed by roughly equal parts of garbage, gasoline fumes, and the exudations from the naked human body under heat.

At seven-thirty, as instructed, I pulled into the Shell service station at the south end of the promenade and paid five francs for parking the Renault 16TS I'd rented from the Avis agency in Cannes. It was a fast car, in good shape but unpretentious in appearance; it should make the Spanish border before dawn, losing itself untraceably in the vast mainstream of the Costa Brava tourist traffic. Taped under its dashboard rode the little Air weight Cobra. I didn't expect to need it, but if I was wrong about that it would probably be needed in the car.

My first surprise turned out to be Miss Yuri Franklin, somewhat overdressed in a blue denim playsuit with a matching cap and sandals, who popped up beside me on the ramp between the service station and the promenade. ". . . You look cross with me, Steve Harvester."

"What are you doing here?"

"Didn't you notice? I was right behind you, all the way from Cannes." She gestured nonchalantly at a taxi driving off, dismissed. "I've known all day that there was something bothering you."

"Yes, there is."

She took my arm, confidently. "I want to help."

"What's bothering me," I said coldly, "is exactly that."

The situation was ridiculous, of course. I had arrived that very moment from a long and angry quarrel aboard *Miss Virginia*. It had been obviously necessary to tell Lita we were leaving, and she'd sensed the reason. She'd insisted on the details, and she had demanded that I take her with me then and there —she, too, wanted to "help," until I'd managed to explain that she'd be dangerously handicapping me instead.

Yuri was saying: "I'm not doing this for money."

"Fine. We understand each other. You're *not* doing this. For five thousand Swiss francs a month."

"But I . . ."

"Good night, Miss Franklin. There are other taxis, over there."

She didn't even hesitate. Her arm tightened on mine as she began to lead me up the ramp. This was my day for being walked by women, like a poodle. "I don't care," she told me, "if it costs me five thousand Swiss francs a month. I'm going with you. You're in trouble of some kind, Steve Harvester."

It was impossible to keep from laughing at her. "The only trouble will be finding someone I'm supposed to meet."

"Who is he?"

"He's a Frenchman. Calls himself Jean-Claude."

"Then let's go find him."

Never let them make you laugh. Already we were wading through the mob that stagnated the boardwalk like an overloaded sewer. "Does His Royal Majesty approve of this?"

"I haven't asked him. He's in church. It's one of those Greek-Orthodox occasions. He'll be out all night. What does this Frenchman look like?"

"Like about five hundred other Frenchmen we've already passed." I was exaggerating, but not very much. There were a great many young men about, and most of them had fancy hairstyles, hairline mustaches, and angry ferret faces.

"But you'll recognize him when you see him?"

"Probably." I doubted it, but I was reasonably sure that he would recognize me, and that he would have objections to my self-elected company. "What *you* must recognize, Miss Franklin, is that he and I have something to discuss that isn't for your pretty ears."

She asked me calmly: "If that's all, why are you meeting him in public? And *please* call me Yuri." Then she saw the towhead little boy confronting her and holding up one hand to stop her like a traffic cop. He had a miniature box camera aimed at her. She posed for him, goodnaturedly, still clinging to my arm; the child triggered his toy and squirted her bare midriff with the water pistol it concealed. Then he ran away, shrieking with pleasure at another victory over a gullible grown-up. "You know, that thing could've been loaded. Someone could have slipped it to the kid and sicked him on to you," I said.

"Loaded? With what?"

"Oh, caustic soda. Acid. Skunk oil. Anything to take you out. The man I'm dealing with won't like your showing up with me."

She suddenly, astonishingly, sounded passionate. "Well, I don't *care*. If you go through with this I'm staying with you."

Right on cue, the street musician we were passing struck up

Tosti's "Serenade," his muted violin cutting the crowd noise like a wire going through a wheel of mildewed cheese. I sneered at him, and at myself, and said: "Go through with what, Yuri? I like you, too, but I don't understand you."

"It's got something to do with those silly college kids," she told me confidently.

". . . It does?"

"They're here, you know. They said they would be, when I talked with them on Monday afternoon, before they left the yacht. They said they had a score to settle with you."

"My dear child, that was two days ago. The stuff they use, their memory doesn't go back that far. Also, their luggage was put on a plane in Málaga, in bond. A New York plane."

"No, Steve. A Paris plane. Air France."

I dropped a coin into the fiddle player's hat. Three very young girls in bikinis, chased by boys, ran screaming into me. Three pairs of hands were everywhere—under my arms, around my hips, between my legs. All of the boys looked like Jean-Claude. They pounced on us and started dragging the three girls and Yuri Franklin off the boardwalk to the beach.

They had no luck with Yuri, who broke loose almost immediately. I could have used the opportunity to ditch her, but I was beginning to get curious. She caught up with me, disheveled and upset. "Those people tried to take me out!"

"I doubt it."

She was clinging to my arm again. "What *were* they after?"

"Probably my wallet."

It was safely buttoned up, of course. In fact, I thought it much more likely that the girls were checking for a gun on me. Yuri said, almost plaintively: "You do know that the kids are making out with that fat Belgian queer, don't you? The one who was at Marcia's party in Tangier?"

"All of them?"

"Well, no. Not exactly. Just the one who's queer himself.

Croup Nichols. But they trust him, and he's helping them."

"With what?"

"You know with what." Again that strange, wise, boyish little grin.

So they had told her everything. Presumably including that Leon de Bas "had something on me." But not just exactly what he was supposed to have. He would have held that back from them. He needed it himself, for keeping me in line.

I wasn't worrying about the Strawberry Preserves Conspiracy, whether they were in France or not, but for the moment this peculiar young Oriental woman did concern me very much indeed. It made no sense at all for her to enter competition for my doubtful favors. Almost as absurd would be whatever notion on her part that she might fool me into thinking she was serious about it. After all, she was a self-proclaimed professional, and evidently a successful one. There were no union rules against it, but the chances of my earning her undying adoration would seem pretty slight. Apparently she had something in mind, something not necessarily to my advantage.

It occurred to me that she might very well be on de Bas's payroll, too. If so, my problems of the evening were liable to escalate. Quite possibly beyond recourse.

By then we'd struggled down the promenade to where it overlooks a cellar patio café with half a dozen Ping-Pong tables. These were all in use, each with their gallery of noisy spectators. The players were young Frenchmen, all of them playing for money. All of them looked like Jean-Claude.

"Is he there?" Yuri asked.

"No," I said. "No, he's not," and guided her away into the crowd, and at that moment someone hissed at me. They hiss at you all over southern Europe, and somehow there's never any real doubt about the sender or the addressee. The sender, in this case, was leaning on the inside rail of the pédalo boatyard on the beach. He didn't look much like Jean-Claude at all. He was an average, middle-aged Frenchman in black swimming trunks. The stencil on his cap and the brass whistle on a cord around his neck would seem to make him an attendant at the yard.

"M'sieu 'Arvestair?" He had the gritty accent of the Marseille slums. "Go to the Luna Park. The candy apple stand." He scowled at Yuri Franklin, shrugged expressively, and added one more word. "Alone."

In that July, the Luna Park was located just off the exit of the boardwalk in Antibes. All it amounted to was a few rides and carnival attractions casually spread over an empty parking lot. It had a tired and raffish air, and correspondingly few customers. The candy apple stand was doing business, but only just enough to keep one woman-server occupied.

Jean-Claude, lounging against the counter, sized up Yuri Franklin with a bilious eye. His English was the kind that has been taught to all the world's Jean-Claudes by Paramount and Warner Brothers over the past four decades. "Who's the bimbo?"

"She's with me. Any objections?"

"It's your funeral."

He slouched away from us into the park. It seemed we were supposed to follow him. Yuri, still clinging to my arm, glanced after him contemptuously. "What's a bimbo?"

"Girl friend. Brooklyn mobster slang, before your time."

"Isn't he something. Where's he taking us?"

"To meet the man you were describing earlier as that fat Belgian queer."

"Whatever for?"

"Well, he's a Soviet agent. He's been bird-dogging my conversations with His Majesty."

"Oh, has he?"

"Yes, indeed. He seems to disapprove."

"I see."

"That sort of thing is usually settled without ladies being present."

"I suppose so," she said thoughtfully. Then, with that oddly boyish little grin, "Let's just assume that I'm no lady."

"Very well, Yuri," I said. "That's any woman's privilege."

Ten yards away, Jean-Claude was talking to the barker of a tent that called itself the *Jardin des Supplices*, or Torture Garden. It displayed the customary gaudy posters advertising the horrific and deliciously immoral cruelties that were to be witnessed within. The barker wore a soiled white dinner jacket but otherwise looked exactly like Jean-Claude. He doubled as the ticket seller, and he had no customers at all just then. He waved us in, impatiently; it seemed we were to be his guests. Jean-Claude himself already walked away from us again, into the entrance grotto crudely fashioned of moss green papier mâché.

Almost immediately he disappeared from sight behind the billowing black curtain at the rear. This, we discovered, opened on a narrow, dimly lighted passage between walls of heavy canvas, ending in a full-length mirror panel operated by a treadle underfoot that swiveled it on groaning hinges and confronted the approaching visitor with a dull, Gothic painting of a man strangling a woman.

"They're playing *games* with us!" Yuri sounded indignant.

"Looks that way," I said. "Want to go home?"

Determinedly she shook her head and pulled my elbow. She had found another curtain that exposed a second passage, at right angles to the first. A prison cage closed this one off, but on inspection the steel bars proved to be painted on a canvas flap. When we pushed through we faced a tattered photorama of a man in the electric chair, complete with treadle-activated sound effects. Jean-Claude continued to play hide and seek with us.

"How campy can they get, Steve Harvester?" demanded
Yuri. ". . . Oh, here's a door!"

I had already found it and was cautiously pushing it ajar. It
had no handle, and it had been set flush in the wall that ended
in the left side of the photorama. This was not a canvas wall, I
noted, but a solidly constructed wooden board fence that went
all the way up to the canvas roof. Behind it, as the slowly moving door revealed, was a vague prospect of considerable space
with a peculiar, irregularly shimmering obscurity like a false
dawn at sea. Yuri walked into it, still tugging at my sleeve, our
feet producing a strange, gritty echo on cement, and then the
lights came on, a double bank of fluorescents overhead, and we
were looking at ourselves again, not in one mirror but in possibly as many as two hundred, placed in rows and in small sets
of different-sized panels covering the wall, including by all
means the door that had slammed shut behind us and had
thereby become unidentifiable.

"So now you know how campy they can get," I said, and
heard the echo bounce my voice around to make it sound like
that of an old woman cackling in Chinese.

A maze of mirrors in a carnival tent isn't a particularly fear-
some place to visit. But if anybody has in mind ripping you off,
he can find lots of less convenient situations. Still, in this case it
seemed fairly obvious that the other side merely wanted to separate us and control our movements. Since that didn't suit my
purpose very well, I kept my back against the wall, using both
hands to probe for seams or hinges.

"Stay right where you are. That door is here somewhere."

The echo chattered *wherewherewhere* at me. Yuri said:
"But you're not supposed to find it. You're supposed to go on
through."

I said I never liked to do what was expected of me. "Hey,
Jean-Claude! Where are you?" That was meant to be a shout,
but the ridiculous acoustics of the place squeezed it into a whis-

per. My unsought companion pulled my sleeve and laughed at me, not very merrily.

"Please, let's get out of here."

She took two steps away from me and bumped into herself. The canted double-mirror panel she confronted seemed to stand alone, but when she tried to grope around it she encountered other panels on both sides. She moved in closer, fumbled for another yard and caught her breath, screamed in distress, and suddenly, completely, violently disappeared from view.

The scream, choked off abruptly, nevertheless kept reverberating for what seemed like a long time. I didn't move until it stopped. Then I said sharply: "Let her go, Jean-Claude. Or there's no deal."

The echo mocked me *dealdealdeal*, but nothing else materialized. I'd already made my mind up about how to cope with the dilemma. I'm as superstitious as most people about breaking mirrors, but you have to be a little flexible about such things once in a while. I shuffled forward, cautiously, and said: "All right, fellows, let's see if this'll get results," and smashed a boot heel through the panel behind which Miss Yuri Franklin had been spirited away.

The jagged hole merely disclosed another empty corridor of mirrors. Two more kicks to clear the shards admitted me to this. When I drew back my foot before another panel, Jean-Claude's image suddenly produced itself in it. He stood behind me to my left, or so it would appear. He did not look especially upset with me.

"*Ça coûte cent francs, monsieur.* A hundred francs, please," he said coldly.

"Where's the girl?"

"After you see Monsieur de Bas, maybe we let her go."

I looked at him and at the empty palm he offered me. "Okay," I said. "A hundred francs it is," and started fumbling for my wallet. When a man agrees to pay you, you're supposed to watch his hands; it shouldn't happen to occur to you that he is misdirecting your attention. I intended to acquire control over *his* movements, and the best way to accomplish that, with his type, was to punt him vigorously in the testicles, Mike Hammer style.

But he had gutter instincts working for him, independent of his eyes. The kick struck his left thigh, high up, less than two inches off. He yelped with anguish, but I hadn't hurt him badly. He was rat-quick, slithering away from me. The knife snicked open, very audibly, before I caught its glitter weaving low, professionally questing for the most convenient entrance-way under my ribs.

I had two problems, one of them the horrible distraction of confronting an infinite number of Jean-Claudes, reflected everywhere. The second problem was a lack of space. If you keep up your homework in the gym, a knife fighter is easy. You attack his front leg, sweeping it from under him by dropping to the floor yourself and pivoting on your left hip. He'll wind up on his tailbone while you follow through the pivot round the compass, kick him smartly in the head, and bounce back to your feet. This sounds much harder than it really is, but it should not be practiced in a narrow corridor between a dozen sets of mirrors with a lot of broken glass lying around.

That left the classic technique of the down blow on the forearm and the three stiff fingers in the solar plexus. This works well, if you don't mind taking a chance or two. The other fellow may be just a little faster than he should be. If he isn't, he may wind up dead, because that finger lance of yours can cause a nerve block that will stop his heart. I didn't want to kill Jean-Claude. I wanted him to take me to his boss. On my terms, not on his.

I backed away from him and said: "*Alors, mon cher ami*, what is this shit? Monsieur de Bas wishes to trade with me, *n'est-ce pas?* I cannot be of service to him if you put that silly toothpick of yours into me."

He made the usual, impractical suggestion for my future sexual behavior and came shuffling after me. I kicked some shards of glass at him, distracting him for the right fraction of a second, clipped him on the arm and in the midriff, pushed him back, and picked the knife up where he'd dropped it on the floor. These little things would have come easier twenty-five years ago, when they were demonstrated to me in the air force. At my current age they made me breathe a little faster than seemed necessary. Also, the chill-acid taste was on my tongue that tells you your adrenal glands are working overtime again.

"The girl, Jean-Claude," I said. "Right now."

I had him by his belt, turned with his back to me, the knife pricking the skin that covered his right kidney. Wobble-kneed, he forced a strangled whinny of discomfort through his throat before he managed to regain enough control to shrug it off.

"It's your funeral, monsieur. This way."

We frog-marched out of there. The maze wasn't as complicated as I thought; it took two turns and twenty steps to reach the exit alley with the funny mirrors that make men look imbecile and women pregnant. My reluctant guide pushed through a side door marked *Privé—Défense d'Entrer* into a storeroom lighted by a single naked bulb. Miss Yuri Franklin had been casually dumped among the packing crates and cleaning supplies. They had trussed her arms and ankles, and they'd made a gag out of her jaunty denim cap. Her glossily styled raven locks sprawled in disorder. She was crying, and she made as persuasive a picture of a savory young female in distress as I had ever come upon.

The ticket seller of the *Jardin des Supplices* lounged back in a decaying armchair. I'd assumed already that he'd closed up shop. He made no move as we walked in—he simply stared at us, complacently. It seemed to take him a long time to realize that trouble was at hand.

Jean-Claude's car proved to be an elderly Peugeot with dirty, imitation-sheepskin seat covers that failed to make up for the broken springs. A miniature toy monkey dangled over the windshield by a rubber band, and to the dashboard had been taped a picture of a toddler on a tricycle, encased in plastic with a printed caption: *sois pas pressé, papa!* Don't hurry, daddy.

"Family man, hmm?"

He managed to ignore me. We were on a narrow local road that climbed into the coastal mountains behind Cannes. The well-known French philosophy on road construction—let them watch the scenery and make them sweat—was very much in evidence. Jean-Claude was duly sweating at the wheel; he had to turn it every few seconds, all the way. The night was hot. So was the wheezing engine, laboring in second gear without respite. The Luna Park was somewhere way down there among a hundred thousand multicolored pinpricks flickering and blinking back at us.

The ticket seller who might be Jean-Claude's twin brother had been left securely tied up on the storeroom floor. His battered armchair was now occupied by Yuri Franklin. I'd removed the gag and readjusted the few yards of packing cord on her to make her less uncomfortable.

"Steve Harvester, what are you *doing?*"

"My dear child, that's pretty obvious."

"You're not taking these off?"

"Just making sure you don't start playing tag with me again. Don't worry, I'll be back to turn you loose."

"But I want to *help.*"

"This way you will." She was bewildered and distressed with me, it seemed. For my part, the decision had been close. I wasn't very much concerned about her witnessing what I intended. The effect on her might have been salutary, and she was in no position to cause legal trouble for me. On the other hand I was determined to prevent all possibility of her once more getting under my feet.

The ferret-faced young Frenchman whose job was supposed to be to take me to de Bas and to keep me in line while I was there needed no further thought, as far as I could see. His leg hurt, and his stomach, and his arm—he winced almost continuously, driving. He had watched me throw the knife away after I'd gone over him carefully for secondary weaponry. It would have made him very happy to take care of me, by inches, but he was apparently too realistic to put any money on the odds. *Sois pas pressé, papa* . . . In turn, I had no reason for displeasure with him. He was useful, not just as a guide but as a decoy, for his presence would be likely, as it had before, to make de Bas feel safe with me. At least for long enough to get my hands on him.

"I wish you would explain something to me, Jean-Claude," I said. "Why do you and your friends offer protection to this fat pig of a Belgian? Don't you know he's trying to sell out?" All that got me was a dark, sidelong scowl and a derisive grunt. "No, really, don't you? *Mais je vous assure, mon cher ami.* Monsieur de Bas desires to see his mother. Only we of the American intelligence can make this possible. You understand a little English, do you not?"

The point was one that had considerably puzzled me that afternoon. The conversation in the tailor shop had been in English, and it had been, on de Bas's side, sufficiently explicit to embarrass him if any of his helpful French comrades had overheard and understood. Of course he might have told them in advance that he was simply conning me. But in effect he'd put himself in double jeopardy, for if the merchandise he'd offered me was phony, it was also meaningless. Its quality could be controlled within twelve hours, he'd explained. If it was good, however, he was practically asking for his own people to put him down.

"*Pense bien*, Jean-Claude," I said. "Give it some careful

thought. The man you're dealing with is an important agent of the KGB, no question about that. But he is not a Russian, and his mother has a terminal disease. She has no more than a few days. She's in a hospital in Brussels, under our surveillance. Do you follow me?"

We groaned and whined through two more hairpin turns.

"You're a liar." Actually, he didn't say that. He spoke five or six words, half of which I vaguely recognized as specialized Marseille argot, something about my highly unconventional, private bathroom habits.

Since the point was hardly worth debating with him I just shrugged and said in English, "It's your funeral, my boy. When do we get there?"

He replied by slowing down and gesturing. We were in pine tree country—it was cooler here, and it smelled better, and there were no other cars in sight. Our headlights caught a dirt track and a rustic arrow sign announcing *Mon Repos*, which is what every other Frenchman likes to call his weekend cabin. To negotiate the turnoff it was necessary to drive past it, stop, and back precariously to the cliff side of the road. The track itself, within ten yards or so, achieved an incline that required full throttle in first gear. The cottage came in view by moonlight after a few minutes of laborious and noisy engine effort. It looked small and commonplace, the usual raw timber, imitation Swiss chalet. It made a reasonable and convenient hideout for a man prepared to wait twelve hours while his questionable bona fides were under investigation.

Through the single window fronting on the track a light was showing at what should be table height. The car still had some fifty yards to go when there was quite a change, quite suddenly, in both the color and the brilliance of this light. It flared from a dim yellow to bright red and filled the window for what seemed like a long time before the thunderclap of the explosion slammed into my eardrums. One more elongated fraction of a second passed until the blast itself rocked the Peugeot and shoved it off the track.

You learn never to be surprised, unpleasantly or otherwise. You also learn to take out first the nearest source of danger. Jean-Claude was still struggling with the wheel. I hit him in the neck and flipped him over into the back seat, and slammed the gears into reverse. The car tore itself loose out of the underbrush and slewed through a half-turn, then shuddered backward up the track into the cabin's empty yard.

There were still sounds of cracking wood and tinkling glass around. The front door had been blown away, clear out of sight. The dust and the coarse-nitro fumes were settling, fast enough to let the moon into the room. I stood outside the doorway, looking in and grimacing. It had to be de Bas, of course, there was so much of him by volume on the ceiling and the walls and on the floor, an average-sized human could not have supplied the raw material on view. Remarkably enough, no fire had started. The explosive, probably plastique, apparently had been concealed under the table top, which had been torn up into matchstick bits.

Explosions have to be set off by electricity or chemistry. That usually means a timer or a wire. I saw no wire, but if a timer had been used the shot man would have had to be a wizard. On the other hand, perhaps he had intended to include me. My arrival had been, after all, somewhat delayed.

I ran back to the car and yanked Jean-Claude out of the back seat. He was conscious, but he seemed content to sprawl among the debris in the yard. My boot heel in his stomach didn't seem to bother him.

"*Alors*, you must be disappointed, my dear fellow."

He stared up at me and vaguely shook his head, and the denial somehow was a great deal more convincing than if he'd protested loud and clear. A sudden thought occurred to me. I got into the front seat, found a flashlight in the glove compartment, put the beam under the dashboard near the steering column. Yes, indeed. Someone had very recently installed a new electric switch.

There is a common enough radio fuse used in demolition work. It can be activated from a moving car, at a convenient distance, by a beam just like the one that opens your garage door. I got out again and stood over Jean-Claude. "'Why did you do it, boy?" No answer. This time I brought down my foot to where it hung an inch or so above his eyes. The flashlight beam still caught enough of his expression to reveal that he was worried. "Tell me," I said coldly.

"'. . . My orders, monsieur.''

"Party orders?''

He passed out again. But that had to be it, of course. The local comrades had become suspicious of Leon de Bas, and they'd checked back that afternoon, through channels, and the word had come to stop the music. But don't bother the American. He doesn't have the goodies yet. Just see to it he doesn't get them, and while you're about it, show him what we do about that sort of thing.

And that would signify, incredibly, that there were goodies to be had.

Of course Jean-Claude would have no information about that. I took my foot back, jumped into the car, and started it by rolling down the track in gear. It had a nasty set of brakes that either locked the front wheels with a scream or needed pumping desperately to deliver anything at all, but somehow I got off the mountain with it and into Juan-les-Pins. My Renault rental at the boardwalk service station felt like a Rolls Royce. I drove it round into the Luna Park that still had a few hundred customers somehow, and parked it at the exit of the *Jardin des Supplices*. In the storeroom nothing much seemed to have changed. The ticket seller was asleep and snoring ripely on the floor. Yuri looked more relieved than angry with me when I took the ropes off her. "What *happened?*"

"Nothing much. I saw our Belgian friend. He didn't make it."

"I don't understand."

"Don't you?"

"Do you mean you killed him?" The idea itself seemed not to be especially uncomfortable to her.

"Let's just say that he's not anymore in a position to prevent His Royal Majesty's return to Bucarest."

I'd made it sound unpleasantly sardonic, and she stared at me as if she had been slapped. "You're *angry* with me, Steve Harvester."

"Not really. I'm irritated with myself. Mostly because I've missed a point somewhere along the line."

"What sort of point?"

"Leon de Bas has been a dead man for some time," I said. "He held a grudge that dated back to his experiences in the Congo with United Nations troops. But you can't do that in our line of business. It's unprofessional, and it affects your judgment. You're supposed to be excused for what you do to people on the other side, but only if it's necessary. Flies that buzz your kitchen table you're allowed to swat, not catch and pull their wings."

"He did that?"

I was putting her into my car by then. We left the park and hit the busy coastal highway back to Cannes. She sat watching me, her shapely legs pulled up seductively into the roomy bucket seat. I was a little old for her, but under different circumstances I'd have done something about her. Experts always are worth cultivating. As it was, I wanted something else from her. "You mentioned those four college kids," I said. "They're still in town?"

"They were this morning. Mick and Val passed by just before you did, on the boulevard."

"Know where they're staying?"

She supplied the information readily. It wasn't more than a five-minute ride. "The trouble with Leon de Bas," I said, "was that he didn't even try to think. He seems to have got by for years, acting on his deplorable emotions. Recently, our side made up its mind to take him out, which was to have been Wahlstrom's job in Tangier. Wahlstrom failed, but the next man wouldn't have fooled around."

"Is that what happened?"

"No. Apparently his own side handled it. It looks like they were justified. What worries me is that he must have realized they'd put him down if they found out."

This time she sounded rather sharply puzzled. "If they found out what?"

"What he was up to. So it follows, logically, that what he was up to couldn't really have been anything subject to Moscow's disapproval. Yet it seems it was."

"But then . . . ?" Yuri threw up her hands. Innocent curiosity had turned into helpless confusion, it appeared. I smiled for her, perhaps a trifle cynically, as we turned into the parking lot of the motel she'd named.

It was a branch of one of the big chains that lately had been on a building spree in tourist areas from Stockholm down to Capetown. It looked just like all the other ones back home—the double-storied wings of blue- and orange-painted rooms, the swimming pool, the office building with a coffeeshop in it, the gaudy neon lights, the sign that said No Vacancy. I parked and leaned back from the wheel. "You did say that those suitcases were shipped in bond from Málaga to Paris, didn't you? Not to New York?"

"That's what the kids told me. They said they'd been advised to go that route."

"Well, let's go see if they're still here themselves," I said.

The night clerk seemed to think so and supplied a number.

At the blue and orange door that bore it I stood back, just out of sight, against the wall. The lights were on behind the curtained window. "Do you mind?"

Yuri wrinkled her pretty nose at me, a little scornfully, and rang the bell. Footsteps came hurrying; the door swung wide. Croup Nichols sounded something less than overjoyed. ". . . Oh! Hello, Miss Franklin."

"Hi! Where's everybody?"

"They've gone on to Paris."

"Without you?" She was persuasively astonished.

"I . . . promised a friend I'd stay tonight."

His hesitation sounded more inspired by a reluctance to communicate than by embarrassment. I took my shoulders off the wall and stepped into the doorway to confront him. "Look who's here," I said. "Hello, Nichols. We want to talk to you about your friend." He'd caught his breath, backing away from me. He wore cream silk pajamas and a matching robe embroidered stylishly with miniature classic motorcars riding across his chest. The room seemed to be one of two connecting studio bedrooms. Its divan beds had been pushed together, made up for the night, with a cold supper laid out on the sideboard featuring a bottle of champagne.

"Planning a party, were you?"

He was staring at me, frightened but defiant. I had kicked the front door shut and followed him into the room until he'd backed against the nearest bed. Behind me, Yuri Franklin giggled musically at my silly question. She was right, of course. We hadn't come here to discuss the obvious.

Still, this was really the first time I'd stopped to contemplate the boy. On previous occasions he had struck me as irrelevant, a complete ninny. The relationship between him and Leon de Bas had hardly seemed to call for second thoughts. There's so much casually farfetched buggery around these days, particularly in this business, you just don't pay attention to it anymore. You take advantage of it when you have to, but the notion that you're into something worth considering, such as a human being with emotions and with qualities of character, however dubious, doesn't readily occur to you. Basil "Croup" Nichols would be about twenty years of age. His tone and mode of speech suggested an Atlantic seaboard college background. He was clean shaven, conventionally handsome, wore his pale blond hair in a long bob he had a way of tossing girlishly. His eyes were cornflower blue, fretful, insecure, but reasonably bright.

I poked a fingertip at him and said: "Let me explain something to you, huh, fella? Those two suitcase loads of junk aren't any use to you in Paris. They're not even worth much more there than you paid for them. Mick knows that much, so he must have in mind forwarding them from Paris to New York in bond. Now aren't you guys aware that you can't get your hands on them without a customs officer examining them? Don't you realize what's going to happen to you then?"

I'd made him happy. I was turning out to be a real square oldtimer after all. He actually smiled at me.

"Shit man, they're not going to *be* examined in New York."

"That right? How come?"

He tossed his pretty hair. "Oh, I'm not laying *that* on you, man."

"So it's all arranged, huh? Not a thing to worry about?" He just stared at me, contemptuously. I glanced at the champagne supper on the sideboard. "Your friend has fixed it up already? Nothing more to do, no phone calls to be made by him? No little notes to write or anything?" Croup Nichols shook his head in wonder. I was even more squared out than he'd imagined. "Yeah, well, that's okay then," I said cheerfully, and turned away toward the door.

Yuri was staring at me, pretending consternation. She'd picked up her cue all right. "But Steve . . ."

"Yeah?"

"Aren't you going to tell him?"

I glanced back at Croup, who hadn't moved or changed expression. "Tell him what? Oh, that his friend is dead, you mean? Now why should he be interested?"

Nothing is so utterly convincing as the truth, dispensed contemptuously. Croup Nichols suddenly looked very young. He closed his eyes and stumbled, weaving. I intended letting him fall down, but he recovered, trying visibly to brace himself. I shrugged at Yuri, for his benefit, and said: "You just don't understand these queens. They're always waiting for another streetcar. This one had already taken him where he was going."

Croup retched violently, clapped a hand over his mouth, and ran into the bathroom. Yuri Franklin, glancing after him, produced a cigarette case from her bag. I snapped my lighter for her; it was the first time I'd seen her smoke. "Golly, you hit him hard," she said uneasily.

"Maybe not hard enough," I said. "I like his story. I want all of it."

The sound of running water reached us, not the sudden cascade from the toilet tank but the sustained eruption of the bathtub faucets. I was pretty slow reacting to it. Probably there'd been at least five seconds of it when the doubtful possibility of Croup taking a bath just then occurred to me.

He'd locked the door, of course. I didn't even try the knob. My boot heel was the quickest passkey to be had. It got me in without delay, and there he was, all right, kneeling beside the tub with a straight razor lying open on the tiles beside him. Both his wrists were rhythmically pumping under water, but he hadn't managed well enough to keep from messing himself up. The jaunty little Packards, Duesenbergs, and Bearcats on his robe had disappeared in blood.

Two tourniquets and a fast ambulance had kept Croup Nichols going with about thirty seconds' margin. I'd been standing by his bed at Cannes Sisters of Mercy, watching him soak up the plasma like a human sponge. Even his eyes had faded to a washed-out lime shade. They stared up at me, identifying me but not reacting to me. "Come on, fella. Hit the ball. You're staying in the game."

The French nun in attendance disapproved of me. I didn't care, but she'd already asked me twice to go away, and she looked ready to start pushing me. The lad himself might need all night to get his brain cells back in operation. Then he might not have the answers I was looking for.

I'd walked away from him. In the solarium Yuri Franklin, waiting for me, seemed to read my thoughts on sight. She looked and sounded more disturbed than I'd have estimated necessary. "Steve, you don't imagine . . ."

"What?"

"Nothing." She took my arm and let me shepherd her into the elevator. "Those two suitcases. You're sure they're packed with *drugs*, aren't you?"

"No, I'm not sure of anything," I said. "Why do you ask?"

"No reason in the world."

"Go on. You can do better."

But she only chewed her lips in evident dismay. I didn't like that very much. She wasn't, after all, supposed to have the slightest knowledge of Leon de Bas's proposition. In the car she said, at last: "It just doesn't make sense. Why should Croup Nichols try to kill himself because you might prevent him and his friends from smuggling a few thousand dollars' worth of hash?"

I told her she was right about that, but that I was in no doubts whatever as to the boy's motive. Homosexual relationships between the very young and the mature are usually strictly mercenary, but when they are not they can be shattering, emotionally overwhelming, for a while. The suitcases were something else, I said. There was no point in her concern about them. What I wanted her to put together was one Carol

Rudolf Ferdinand von Hohenzollern-Sigmaringen, *soi-disant*. For five thousand Swiss francs per month. No, I was definitely not upset with her. I just expected her to stay with what we had agreed upon.

She'd sulked until we stopped under the porte cochere of the Château Lucardi. Then she had tried one more fast and skillful pass. It's quite a curiosity how relatively helpless the male animal turns out to be when the experienced female takes him on. I would have managed, somehow, but not easily or gracefully. Not without Marcia Ellis strolling out on the portico at exactly the right moment.

"Steve, darling, *there* you are! I thought you had already left for Spain. . . . Oh, I'm *so* sorry, my dear, did you drop your *handbag* on the floor? His Majesty should be here soon. Prince Sturza telephoned from church a little while ago for the chauffeur."

"He must have missed me," Yuri estimated coolly. "Thank you so much for protecting me, dear Marcia. Good night, Steve Harvester. It's been an education." She was out of the Renault and through the front door in a flash of tawny legs.

I'd started to get out myself, a trifle clumsily under the circumstances, but my hostess waved me back behind the wheel. "You must be *anxious*, Steve dear."

"Must I?"

"Well, she *is* rather a forward child, isn't she? And with you already *carrying* water on both shoulders."

"She's unfinished business," I said. "But I can't spare the time just now. Hang on to her, please, Marcia, I'll be back in a few days. Don't make a place for her in your collection, not before you check with me."

That got me nothing but a cagey grin from where she stood beside me, looking down on me and showing half her age in coral dress pajamas by Dior. Twenty-two years is quite a while for any man and woman to stay friends, outside a really successful marriage. I grinned back at her, nudged the gearshift, and slid out into the driveway and away from there. The yacht harbor was less than ten kilometers away, and most of them downhill.

It offered me a vacant parking slot between the mooring bollards holding *Miss Virginia* in her berth. The glamorous white frigate slept under a waning moon; only her gangway light was showing. On the boat deck, standing by the rail, Lita de Vargas watched me walk across the tarmac of the quay. She didn't wave or turn to face me when I joined her. She wore slacks and a light sweater, traveling clothes, as she'd been instructed.

"We're not leaving. Not tonight."

She didn't even glance at me. "You rotten bastard," she said coldly.

"Why is that?"

She told me why. She had been waiting for me. On the boat deck. For an hour and a half she'd been convinced that I was dead. The telephone . . . Oh, of course! I had been busy. That was different. That certainly made everything all right.

I said I'd simply failed to realize that she'd be worrying as much as that about me. Hadn't I explained to her before I left that I could handle it, no problem? Which was how it had turned out.

"You've killed him?"

She was speaking in an undertone, so low and flat I barely understood her. She seemed terribly upset, much more so than the circumstances warranted. Something I didn't know about was bothering her badly. It would have to wait until I got my homework done. "Go to your room, please. I'll be down in a few minutes. Everything is fine."

She flinched as if I'd slapped her face. She almost ran away from me, almost fell down the ladder to the promenade deck. I stared after her in sharp astonishment. She was a sportswoman, with excellent reflexes, thoroughly coordinated. She had not been drinking. Nothing should be capable of doing this to her. I set my teeth and strode into the radio shack, told the Pakistani operator what I wanted, and sat down behind the desk.

He had a dockside phone connection plugged into his board. I could have asked him to relay the call down to my cabin, but there was no point in that, he could have listened anyway. In New York City it was 8 P.M., the previous evening. The duty officer responded with his number, recognized my voice, identified it electronically, and took thirty seconds to put Jimmy Dexter on the line. He sounded brisk with me, the millionaire television packager disturbed at home, probably needlessly. "You've sold the program to our Belgian clients?"

"No, sir. There were two objections. They don't care about the story line. They liked the actor, but not in this part, just as I thought they would."

"Well, are they casting him for what they have in mind?"

"He had a contract with another company," I said. "But it was canceled, earlier this evening."

The silence at his end was punctured by his grandchildren, somewhere in the near-background, getting into mischief. He ignored them. "If you're sure about that," he said carefully, "we might be interested." I said I'd assumed as much, but that the script seemed pretty controversial to me. That, he told me, was the point. If it was controversial, the network wouldn't go for it, of course. "How do the Belgians feel about that part of it?"

I said I'd have to call them to find out, but that they'd probably agree with me.

"That's not quite good enough." He must have clapped a hand over the phone and called the kids to order; they were quiet when he came back on. ". . . It'll have to be determined, one way or another. You can see that, can't you, Harvester?"

I said I could, and promised to determine it, and got the

Cannes long-distance operator back. Her Brussels line was open, but she had a little trouble with the private number at the other end. It answered, finally, with an exasperated bass growl, when I gave my name. "Christ, fella, what a time you picked. Get back to me in half an hour." I said I might be on a plane in half an hour. "So get back to me tomorrow. What I'm into here has to be taken care of now."

I said the point was that I couldn't wait to meet the people he was sending down, they'd have to be recalled in any case, the matter had been settled. He knew what I meant all right. He swore at me, extravagantly. "You terminate him, buster?"

"No, sir. They did."

"Yeah? You sure?" He reconsidered briefly when I didn't answer. "Aah, the hell with it. We lose a little business. Now what's so fucking urgent about that?"

I said I'd been instructed to explore the reason. What if I should come up with this Dancing Dog he'd heard about?

"Buy him a hamburger."

"Okay, colonel," I said. "I'll do that. If you're satisfied."

But he'd already slammed his phone back on the hook.

DETERMINATION

PARIS, THURSDAY, JULY 22.

The press relations office at Orly has been tucked out of sight on the third floor of the administration building between two employees' washrooms, in a corridor the public doesn't use. I'd known about it since my first Paris assignment, in the early Fifties, when they'd given me a press card from a syndicate that specialized in motion picture news. You get a great deal of cooperation asking questions that supposedly have something to do with a movie in production or a star in trouble. Everybody loves you, and nobody worries about you.

At nine o'clock on Thursday morning I was holding up the wall inside the little anteroom that never closes. There are chairs, of course, but they're not very comfortable, and there is a General Electric coffeemaker on the table with the stack of ancient magazines. It doesn't work, but you're expected to appreciate the fact that somebody meant well.

I didn't really manage to appreciate much else just then. At fifty-four, a sleepless night can bend your mind like so much cold spaghetti.

There was also, or there had been, Lita in the night. I'd walked into her stateroom and had found her at the dressing table with its triplex mirror lights full on, intently studying herself. This was, for her, unusual behavior, since I'd always known her to be very sure indeed of what she had. "It's rather foolish, actually, isn't it?" she told me, falsely bright, without a glance at me.

"What is?"

"For us to be concerned about Francisco's disapproval, if he should find out. It couldn't possibly mean all that much to him. D'you realize I shall be thirty-six next month?"

"You'll need a face lift almost any day now," I said stupidly.

"Yes, that's what that French doctor said to me this afternoon. Not in so many words, but he explained that it's quite late in life for me to have a child. You know, I think Francisco wouldn't pay any attention. He'd expect me not to come back to Colombia, of course, but why should he be interested otherwise in some old bag who let herself get knocked up by her Yanqui gigolo?"

"Well, very good," I said. "You understand the general much better than I do. Would you suggest we notify him as a matter of, uh, courtesy? Or shall we let him find out for himself?"

The cool green lilac eyes ignored me. They seemed ruthlessly intent on where a fingernail explored imaginary crow's feet. "I was twenty when he married me, you know."

"You've mentioned it. Let's face the situation as it stands. Leon de Bas is gone, turned off by his own people. Before I could get my hands on him. It's possible that he communicated with your husband, to create a problem for me or just out of malice, but I doubt it. I was useful to him, or he thought I was. Which means for now we only have to worry about Ana and Jacinto. They won't bother us for a few days. Marcia agreed to keep them busy at the château."

"But you said we weren't leaving for Spain tonight." She'd suddenly become aware that I had something else in mind.

"Maybe tomorrow night we can. De Bas left me a legacy in Paris."

"You're *going?*" She'd come to her feet and swung around on me. The lilac eyes were wide with disbelief.

"No other way. It almost has to be a put-on. But I promised to make sure. You'll call the doctor for the test results tomorrow afternoon?"

Before I'd finished talking I knew that was it, that nothing else could possibly have hit her quite so hard. She didn't even try to find the words for it. She faced me, with her eyelids fluttering now to contain the tears that welled behind them. "There is no need."

I just managed to bite back a grunt of dismay. *"When did it happen?"*

". . . About an hour ago. While I was waiting for you on the boat deck. It was—different from what I've been accustomed to."

She came into my arms for shelter from her grief. I had to brace against a curiously light-headed sense of disappointment. Words formed in my throat and were suppressed before articulation. Nothing I could say would serve to comfort her or reassure myself. So it was she who spoke, uncertainly, at last. "You wanted it?"

"Yes. Yes, I did."

"I can't go back to him. Not anymore. I won't."

"All right."

"Must you still go to Paris?"

"Only for a day or so."

The Air France press relations girl walked in at twenty minutes after nine. She wore a micro-mini dress, no bra, no hosiery, and a sophisticated upsweep of her waist-long chestnut hair. She looked absurdly young, and very French, and more than half-annoyed with me for being there ahead of her.

She knew enough to diagnose my nationality. " 'Ave you been waiting long?"

"Just twenty minutes."

"I am not suppose' to be here before ten o'clock," she told me irritably and, I was inclined to estimate, untruthfully. Her accent came off pretty bad. She probably was temporary help, a substitute during the *grandes vacances.* She unlocked the office door, tossed her handbag on the desk, and dropped into the swivel chair behind it. There were other chairs. Presumably I saw them and was free to take one if I wished. She didn't really notice if I did or not, or if I'd even followed her into the room. She got a cigarette going with one hand and an interoffice number dialed with the other in three seconds flat. The number answered, and she went into a rattle of discussion that I was expected to assume to be about official business.

I put a finger on the interrupter bar, depressed it, and said conversationally, in French, that I was in a hurry. It took a few moments for her to become aware of what had happened.

"You are what?"

"This is a press card, *chère mademoiselle.* I'm sure you have seen one or two of them before. Perhaps your girl friend will consent to talk about her double date with you last night after you've done a little work for me."

She banged down the receiver, jerked the card out of my hand, and stared at it. "The Hermes Agency? *Connais pas.*"

"That's all right." I wasn't mad at her, just in no mood to play her game. "Let's call the airport manager, shall we? He also doesn't know the Hermes Agency, but he'll be happy to explain your duties to you. On the phone or in his office."

"He is on vacation, Monsieur 'Arvestair," she said maliciously and gave me back my card. I shrugged, picked up the phone, and turned her Roladex around to riffle through it for the number. This time it was she who put her finger on the bar. "*Qu'est-ce que vous voulez, monsieur?*"

"A matter of no great importance. I am interested in three passengers to New York, probably Air France, perhaps another carrier. Here are the names. They may have left last night, but they're more likely to have booked a flight today."

She glanced at the half-sheet of notebook paper I'd put on the blotter of her desk. "What is the nature of your interest in them?"

"They're a young actors' group returning from a European tour. I want to interview them."

That, to judge by her expression, was more like it. She got on the phone again and came up with the answer in no time at all. "I'm sorry, Monsieur 'Arvestair. They left at midnight on Air France Flight 28. They landed in New York an hour and a half ago."

"All three of them?"

She checked her notes. "Mademoiselle Valerie Gardner, Messieurs Michael McGowan and George Johnson. *Oui*, monsieur, all three of them."

I thanked her and walked out, presumably as much to her relief as mine. It was bad news, of course, but I was hardly through. The customs pound for passengers' effects in bond, at Orly, is a relatively small affair established in a basement corner. From the sous-chef's glass-enclosed cubicle there is a view of a few dozen storage shelves, most of them empty, and a single, horseshoe-shaped inspection stage. The sous-chef was in uniform, and his magnificent, white cavalry mustache suggested he was crowding his retirement age. The information I was looking for is publicly available, but he was curious about me anyway. "You are of the American police, monsieur?"

"I am a journalist."

"*Ah, ça.* But certainly." He disbelieved me, but he didn't care. "Two suitcases, you say, *monsieur le journaliste.* From Málaga, in Spain, via Air France, shipped on the nineteenth or the twentieth." He ran the butt end of a pencil stub along the margins of his register. It stopped and indicated for my benefit the entry that showed *2 valises consignées à M. Michael J. McGowan* had been duly claimed on Wednesday, July 21. I asked him if he could remember the transaction, but he shook his head. "I was off duty yesterday, monsieur."

"This baggage was inspected by your colleague?"

"But of course, monsieur. Or it could not have left the entrepôt."

They even had a note of Mick McGowan's passport number, made when he'd identified himself. I shook my head, trying to clear it. There were three possible explanations: negligence and bribery seemed the most likely two of them, in which event it would be pointless to try questioning the douanier involved.

Three explanations. It was number three I cared for least of all.. What if these bags had been examined properly, and nothing dutiable had been found in them?

Problem: You are Leon de Bas. In Tangier. You have learned about a scheme to smuggle something nasty into the United States. You want to sell this valuable information, on short notice, but the timing is important. What you need is a technique to pin that down.

Any suggestions, class?

Please, sir, I know a way. I'd ask the people who set up the scheme to let me use it, as a favor.

How, Stevie?

Oh, sir, that's easy. I would tell them I had friends who'd like to take some hash into New York. Then I would make some friends, such as the Strawberries, and put ideas into their minds. Maybe I'd have to promise them a little money. But I'd work it out so that my shipment would be going in on the same order with the nasty one. Then, if you bought my information, I'd describe my shipment to you, and what I'd been told to do with it.

That's very clever, Stevie. And your shipment needn't really have any hash in it at all.

Oh, no, sir. Why take any chances with the Spaniards or the French? They're rough on drugs. *Tell Brussels that I will reveal to you, tonight, the mechanism of the conduit, and its operators. They will have twelve hours to control my information* . . .

I'd left the customs pound by then. The Strawberries were on Flight 28, due in New York about two hours ago. If that was it, if something had been rigged for the arrival of that one specific flight, forget it. That would be the ballgame, if there really was a ballgame. But de Bas had said twelve hours. From last night. Say ten o'clock last night, since he would reasonably have allowed some time for us to meet, and haggle, and for me to get back to a phone.

My watch said five minutes past ten, right now.

I shook my head. Any more bright ideas, class? Well, sir, after all, Mr. de Bas was *anxious* to do business with you. He wouldn't try to cheat you at this point, because he'd only cheat himself. So if the Strawberries were on Flight 28, like the nice lady said, maybe their luggage wasn't.

Thank you, Stevie.

There's another luggage store room I had come across before, on the same basement lobby as the customs pound. This one's a good deal larger and more active, with three airline employees sorting and stacking, loading and unloading trolleys, checking manifests. A sign proclaims *Défense d'Entrer—No Entrance.* I strolled casually by and hung about, watching one of the clerks move two identical white plastic suitcases from a low shelf into a trolley. He was having trouble lifting them, I noticed. Evidently they were heavier than might have been expected for their size. At least a dozen counterculture stickers covered each of them. Mostly these were the common ankh and daisy labels, but one suitcase had been bumper-stripped AMNESTY NOW. Its mate displayed DUCK DIRTY DICK, just like the Volks bus in Tangier.

The clerk, already trundling off with them, glanced up with

understandable annoyance when I stopped him and inquired about their ownership. "They are not yours, monsieur."

"They look like mine."

He stared at me. The French are undisputed champions of the world in the suspicious stare, but this young Frenchman wasn't merely skeptical. He knew, for reasons not yet clear to me, that I was conning him. He casually, much too casually, checked the clipboard he was carrying. "Your name, monsieur?"

Both suitcases had Air France destination tags marked JFK clipped to their handles. Neither tag showed up the flight number that is supposed to be scrawled on by the check-in attendant. I turned one of them around, and there it was: FLT 28, struck off and substituted by FLT 101. I gave the clerk my best production of an artless smile and said, "You're right, these don't belong to me. Lost luggage, aren't they?"

"This is the department of lost luggage, monsieur. There is no admission to the public."

He was definitely more unhappy with me than the circumstances warranted. I walked away from him into the corridor and turned around. He was still watching me. I waved goodbye to him like just another simple-minded tourist and continued on my way; once out of sight I sprinted for the elevators to the main floor, caught one that came close to amputating my left foot, raced for the locker that contained my overnight bag, pounded back across the lobby to the transatlantic counter of Air France. The clock behind it saw me coming and deliberately moved its minute hand from 10:18 to 10:19. Flight 101, said the departure board, would take off at 10:35 for JFK, and it would be On Time.

NEW YORK, THURSDAY, JULY 22.

Intuition is a dangerous and tricky business. If you depend on it, the law of averages will pull you down. It has to. Nobody's that sensitive. Professional clairvoyants and some ESP subjects can hit the button three times out of five, but you don't catch them betting any money on those odds.

For slightly more than seven hours I'd had a splendid opportunity to contemplate this fundamental truth which, incidentally, would not have been accepted by my Navajo great-grandmother in Santa Fé.

The jumbo jet was overbooked, and took off forty minutes late. I'd managed to get on it in one of those last-second confusions at the gate, no doubt depriving someone with a perfectly good reservation of his first-class seat. My conscience might have bothered me some other time about that, but on this occasion there were just too many reasons why I couldn't sleep, and one of them was that my memory persisted in replaying a comparatively unimportant happening in Algiers in December, 1942.

That summer Maryanne and I had lost the baby, and I'd been washed out of fighter pilot training. In July, the air force, for no special reason, put me into what was known at that time as S.1 and often since has been reorganized and renamed and consolidated. The detachment of it that went to North Africa with Eisenhower was composed of half a dozen first lieutenants, one of them myself, and twenty-odd enlisted men. We had the job of catching German agents and Vichy collaborators. So did everybody, from the FBI on down. There were so many of us, we were always trying to arrest each other's undercover spooks.

On Christmas Day, at the inevitable frozen turkey dinner, somebody had brought a British guest. The officers' mess was on Rue Voltaire in what had been a private school for girls. It housed and fed commissioned personnel from various minor air force headquarters, loosely affiliated, such as censorship, judge advocate, police administration, and our own. The Englishman wore RAF blues, two and a half stripes, and was the only man in sight to display wings. He had the usual Battle of Britain mustache, ginger-brown, with matching hair as long as mine is now, which in those days was hardly typical. His decorations started with a triple DFC.

There was no reason in the world why I should have been interested in him. He was at a table forty feet away, with majors and lieutenant-colonels in his lap. I wondered later if I'd only noticed him and managed to resent him because he'd accomplished something I had failed. The fact remains that halfway through the meal I put my second glass of wine down, walked across the mess, and spoke to him without so much as introducing myself or acknowledging the presence of superior officers.

"Mind showing me your i.d., squadron leader?"

He was in his thirties, and he had the weathered-brick complexion of the seasoned soldier. He looked up at me and at the vacant bosom of my battle jacket with a courteously doubtful eye. His drawl was pure Oxonian. "Of course I shouldn't mind, old boy. Why do you ask?"

"I don't have to explain my reasons to you, sir," I told him.

I was twenty-three, and suffering my first Intuition. Everybody at the table stared at me in disbelief, and one of the light colonels said, impatiently: "Don't make a horse's ass of yourself, will you, Harvester. Just go away."

"Sorry, sir. I'm within my rights."

Somebody snorted. Someone else demanded: "Is he?" The light colonel, scowling, said I was and waved me off. The RAF flier continued to look owlishly at me and at my hand, palm up under his nose. At last he shrugged and started to reach for his wallet, snapped a finger and said, "In my coat, old boy."

"Will you come with me, sir?"

The man who'd brought him stumbled to his feet. He was a retread major in the Service of Supplies who supervised this mess and six or seven like it. He had very visibly been diving in the jug. He clapped an arm around my shoulders. He was a good fellow. So was I. So was his guest. Why spoil everybody's Christmas dinner? I stepped out of his embrace and said I wasn't the one spoiling it.

Somebody told me to go out into the hall and find the coat. The RAF man said that was scarcely necess'ry, old boy, thanks awfully, he'd go for it himself. He took his eyes off me, got up, and walked away. When he was in the doorway to the hall, he glanced over his shoulder. His expression was composed, almost complacent. That was a mistake. He knew that I was right behind him, so he should have been annoyed with me. Not greatly, but enough to show.

He realized it when he saw me reaching for the strap across the holster on my belt. He tried to slam the door on me. It bounced off my left foot, but he was fast: he got across the hall and halfway down the corridor that would have taken him into a back yard opening into a maze of private gardens. I yelled after him, something that was supposed to sound like "Halt!" just as they'd told us during training at Orlando. What they really wanted us to shout was, "Halt, security police," but they admitted we might not have time. The pistol was an Army .45 I didn't like, as noisy as a bomb, indoors, and much too power-ful. I fired it at his legs, and he turned cartwheels like a circus acrobat, and smashed into the back door, and transformed him-self into a stack of blood-soaked laundry. When the medics got to him they said I'd hit a thigh bone, and the slug had ranged around and up into the pelvis, disemboweling him. He was not a German agent. He was an Italian bomber pilot with a British college education who'd been shot down on a local raid the night before. The uniform he'd sneaked out of its owner's billets, hoping it would help him to escape. It didn't, but it might have if a boozily hospitable American hadn't insisted on buying his Christmas dinner.

Or if my intuition had been less dependable, that time.

Spotting those suitcases at Orly was, of course, another mat-ter altogether: partly it had been a lucky break, and partly the peculiar instinct you acquire with thirty years' experience in al-most any trade, the instinct that will put you somewhere in the way of lucky breaks. But the decision to get on that plane, at any cost, had been intuitive. I wasn't even happy about it, or happy with myself. I didn't want to lose two days out of my life by going to New York. I didn't care about the Strawberry Preserves Conspiracy and whether they could get away with bringing in a load of drugs, or Dancing Dogs. If there was such a thing, our people in New York could easily have taken care of it, given the lead, by telephone, that my so-called intu-ition seemed to be so terribly intent for me to follow up myself.

The charming, overburdened stewardesses served me lunch at one o'clock, and tried to give me more champagne at five, and at six-thirty or a little afterward, which was one-thirty in the afternoon that summer in New York, Air France Flight 101 came down on JFK. Its four hundred and sixty-some-thing passengers carried me with them in a steady torrent down the corridors of International Building One, past Health and Immigration desks, into the baggage area. I put a foot down on the guard rail of the carrousel and braced myself against the straining herd. The first half dozen of perhaps a thousand suitcases, trunks, parcels, Valpaks, rucksacks, duffel bags, and kiddie carts made their appearance, and the crowd made a collective noise somewhere between a rumble and a groan. Ten minutes of considerable chaos passed. The property of Michael J. McGowan entered and achieved three circuits on the carrousel, admonishing all present to demand AMNESTY NOW and to DUCK DIRTY DICK. No one paid any notice. None of more than seven hundred eager arms reached out for it.

At last a personable young man in the airline uniform approached, a porter with a trolley cart in tow. He waited for an opening, found one, got to the guard rail, hefted the two suitcases, and passed them to the porter. An expensive trunk, brushed pigskin with gold-plated hardware, also seemed to interest him. He got hold of it by one of its three handles, but the moving belt kept dragging it away from him. The porter rescued him and helped him put it on the cart. The pair of them strolled off in the direction of the customs barrier.

I was in line behind them when the customs officer on duty at Aisle Seven waved them through.

There wasn't anything unusual about it. He was just another customs officer, late middle-aged, with a clean shaven Irish face, not stupid, not especially intelligent, not kind, not hard. He looked at me and raised an eyebrow at my little overnight bag. "Afternoon, sir. Is this all you have?"

"I live abroad. I have a business meeting to attend."

He nodded, motioned at the bag for me to open it, poked casually through my toilet articles, waved down the lid, and slapped a sticker on it. I took off with it and hurried after the Air France agent, his porter, and his trolley cart. They had already crossed the customs lobby and were entering a pebbled glass door marked with the word *Private* and the airline's name.

When I caught up with them, inside, the porter was unloading the two suitcases and the brushed pigskin trunk, adding them to a stack of luggage on the shelves that occupied one wall. The agent, with his clipboard under one arm, leaned against the desk to watch him. Both of them looked up at me, not really bothered or surprised. I shouldn't have come in, at least not without knocking, but I was the public. I bought tickets, dispatched cargo, and wrote letters of complaint.

". . . Yes, sir, can I help you?"

He was as American as I, and much more pleasant. "I'm just curious," I said, and gestured at the shelves. "Lost luggage, isn't it?"

"That's right, sir." He was offering a rueful grin. It was expected of him. "All of it."

"Moves right through customs, doesn't it?" I said, appreciatively.

"Well, after all, sir. Smugglers never seem to lose their bags."

I liked him. I was tired, and in a nasty mood, but he was fine. There are a lot of purse snatchers and baby killers who appear to be such nice young men, but not to me, they don't. I've been around too long for that. I nodded at him and looked more closely at the porter. He was just another middle-aged, hard-working black. He had a struggle with the pigskin trunk. It didn't seem to be particularly heavy, but it was a clumsy piece to move. A leather insert with a plastic window on its side contained the owner's card, engraved in flowing cursive script: *Maria de Cardozo, Buenos Aires.*

"That one still has some traveling to do," I said. "Deliver to the customers, don't you?"

"Of course, sir. All the airlines do." The agent had my number now. I was a fellow with a nose problem. That didn't worry him a bit. "It's almost always our mistake, you know," he cheerfully reminded me. I looked at him again, and my expression changed his mind for him. He suddenly wasn't so sure about me anymore. "Is something wrong, sir?"

"Maybe. What if I were working for your company? In Paris. At the airport."

"Yes, sir?"

"I could make mistakes deliberately, couldn't I?"

"But sir, why would you want to do a thing like that?" The agent sounded mildly horrified by now.

"What do you think, my friend?" I said. "Suppose I were a smuggler? Or a communist?"

He winced, quite visibly. He managed some sort of a laugh. "Ha-ha! That's pretty good, sir."

"Yeah, it is."

Even the porter scowled at me. I didn't care. These two were out of it. Only the Paris end would be involved in this. *A conduit into the United States* . . . Somebody had found out, probably years ago, that passengers' lost luggage went through U.S. Customs uninspected, as a matter of routine.

They'd waited until they had something really worthwhile, something that would require, the way Leon de Bas described it to me on the Atalaya Park Hotel beach, very careful timing and security. But at the New York end they didn't need any accomplice working for the airline. They were better off with this nice, unsuspecting boy doing his job.

"If I were you, I'd open one of these," I said, and pointed at the suitcases.

The agent looked at them. "You haven't told me who you are, sir," he reminded me.

"That's right. I haven't."

He assumed I knew what I was doing. People will. He nodded at the porter, who produced the little lock pick they all seem to carry. AMNESTY NOW's locks held out about three seconds.

When its lid came up, we were presented with a view of

about fifty pounds of tattered European magazines and pocket-books, the kind they sell in most North African bazaars for pennies. Both the agent and the porter, upset with me, stared at me.

".... Try the other one."

DUCK DIRTY DICK seemed to be packed with month-old copies of three different Tangiers newspapers in Arabic and French. Something began to quirk the corners of my mouth. I'd offered Mick McGowan sixty thousand dollars for this lot. *No, man. Like, we're in this for fun as much as profit.* As if he could have expected me to pay him without previous inspection of the merchandise.

The porter started to lock up. I handed him a dollar bill and let the agent see my more-or-less-official scowl again.

"All right. Now let's go for the big one."

He just looked confused. I pointed with a thumb at the white pigskin trunk, and on that very instant the two men walked in. They wore the starched, clean whites of ambulance attendants, but they seemed to be in no great hurry, or particularly conscious of the oddness of their presence there. Both of them, by their faces and their accent, would be Spanish or Latin-American. "You have here the lost luggage of Air France, no?"

They just glanced at me in passing, without interest. They'd left the door wide open. I went out, turned back, reentered as if I'd forgotten something. No one noticed me. The center of attention was the pigskin trunk the porter was already dragging off the shelf.

"We'd have delivered it today, you know," the agent said. He sounded just a little hurt, as if his reputation could have been involved.

"It is all right. No problem," said the second man, indifferently.

"Very well, sir. If you'll sign here, please."

The agent made a cross mark on his clipboard with a ball-point pen. The first man took the pen and scrawled with it, returned it, and went back to help his partner. They began to carry off the trunk. They handled it as if it were a stretcher with a body on it. When I stepped aside to let them pass, they carefully ignored me.

Both the porter and the agent watched me shut the door. They didn't like that, and they didn't like my snatching up the clipboard from the desk. The last line on the pad of forms it held said 7/22 FLT 28-FLT 101. Trunk, pigskin, fittings gold. Maria de Cardozo, 1324 West 84th Street, NYC. The signature scrawl was illegible.

"So you were going to deliver it today, were you," I said.

The agent took his board away from me and put it back under his arm. "Maybe you'd better show me something with your name on it, sir," he suggested.

"What would be the point of that?" I asked him. "You can't read." He saw I wasn't joking. He backed off as if I'd cocked a fist at him. "There isn't any thirteen-hundred block in the West Eighties," I reminded him. "That address would be in the middle of the Hudson River. You know that, you're a New Yorker, but you didn't plug your eyes into your memory. Which is another way of saying you can't read, isn't that right?"

The taxidriver seemed to be a Pole from Brooklyn. His police card, framed into the back of the front seat, called him John Zsygmunt, and his bullneck, bullet head, and questionably shaved, square jaw presumably accounted for the fact he hadn't bothered to install the anti-mugger shield that separates most New York cabbies from their customers. He dourly watched the pigskin trunk and the two men in white loading it in their ambulance parked in a red zone fifty yards ahead.

"You know them?"

"Nah. We got a million of 'em."

"Unmarked ambulances?"

"Yah."

"How come?"

"Mister, there's lotsa private places."

"I suppose so. Think you can stay with them?"

He glanced back at me without a word. I'd questioned his professional capacity. The ambulance, a moss-green Cadillac, was getting under way. It hit the parkway in no special hurry, joined the westbound traffic stream, and headed in the general direction of Manhattan, fifteen miles along.

My surly Polish friend drove in the center lane, four cars behind it. Everybody did an easy fifty-five. It was a hot day, nobody was anxious to exert himself, not in the middle of the afternoon. I had to struggle as it was to keep my eyelids up. I wasn't happy with myself at all. The situation left too much to be desired.

There was, of course, no doubt of it that I had something by the tail, quite possibly Leon de Bas's Dancing Dog. But I kept hearing the ferocious chuckle and the heavy gravel bass from Brussels. *Look, fella, the Russkies just don't operate that way. They're gunners, rocketeers—it's gotta be with a big bang, you know?* I didn't know, but the good colonel probably was right. Or he could be distracted by the usual police fixation about modus operandi: hoods with guns don't carry poison. Bet on that, and you might go before your time.

A gun was what I needed, but the Cobra was about four thousand miles away, securely taped under the dashboard of my rented car parked at Nice airport. There had been too many other things to think about.

With time available at JFK, I might have called the office. Jimmy Dexter would have been delighted with me. "This is Harvester. I think I'm into something. I could use a gun. Where am I? Well, I'm going to be in a cab, tailing a private ambulance. It won't be marked, I don't imagine, and its li-cense'll be phony. Yeah, uh-huh, that's right, I've no idea where they are going, what they're taking there, or who they are. We may be on our way to Denver, Colorado. Oh, I see. When I get there, you'd like me to call back. You'll send your secretary with a gun."

In thirty years, this sort of nonsense has to come up every now and then. Most often, guns are not the answer anyway, which was why I'd gone up against de Bas without one although quite resolved to kill him. There is, of course, nothing wrong with killing for a proper reason; obviously war and self-defense are not the only two. The squalid Belgian qualified for both of those. So, very likely, would the people I was dealing with.

Hot afternoon and all, I didn't like their driving. They seemed much too unconcerned, much too relaxed. Even at fifty-five, some of the traffic in their lane was tailgating or passing them. My driver, forced to lag behind, was being passed in turn, sometimes by other cabs whose jockeys stared at him. Presumably he didn't care since he'd been promised fifty bucks over the meter charge, but any changes in the normal flow of traffic on a busy freeway become noticeable pretty soon to anyone who happens to be watching for them.

"Think they've spotted us?"

"Yah."

"Well, let's hope you're wrong. We can't afford to pass them. They would recognize me."

"Whatever you say, mister."

My Polish friend changed lanes and dropped behind a little more. Our quarry signaled for the Queens Boulevard exit. At the stoplight change it turned sedately west again. "They seem to want the Fifty-ninth Street bridge."

"Nah."

"This'll take them to it, right?" I was considering the risk of crossing it ahead of them somehow and catching them at the Manhattan end. There are too many taxis in Manhattan. Nobody can tell if one of them is on a tail job.

"Mister, they'd of saved ten minutes staying on the parkway."

He was probably correct. Queens Boulevard leads straight up to the bridge, but it has six or seven miles of poorly staggered traffic lights. The issue became academic soon enough. The moss-green Cadillac swung off the boulevard and turned into the town of Forest Hills. They have a famous tennis club there, but the place itself is just another New York bedroom suburb, hundreds of short blocks of quiet residential streets. A city cab trying to stay behind an ambulance in Forest Hills is just as inconspicuous as a banana on the counter of a beauty shop. "They seen us, mister."

"Looks like it. Don't lose them, please."

The ambulance turned on its siren and red blinkers, took three corners on two screaming tires, and very nearly hit a housewife in a crosswalk with a baby in her shopping cart. It crashed three stoplights in a row, regained the boulevard, and careened east this time, away from New York City. In no time at all it had cranked up to eighty mph. Ahead of it, Long Island stretched a hundred miles to Montauk Point, and offered something like ten thousand miles of city streets, expressways, country roads, and cow paths.

Traffic on the boulevard obediently cleared the center lane. Of course a siren opens space for more than just one vehicle. My Polish friend had parked a ham-sized forearm on the button of his horn and put his battered yellow Plymouth in the ambulance's wake as if a towing cable were connecting them. The Cadillac was faster, but not very much, and it was less maneuverable—any ambulance has a long wheelbase, and has been designed more for the patients' comfort than for speed. As chases go, this one was pretty nasty just the same. It seemed to last forever, with no end in sight. It roared right through Long Island City and Jamaica into Nassau County. It was physically dangerous as well as thoroughly uncomfortable, and there seemed to be no way of stopping it, no way at all except a really bad accident.

"I'll pay for damages."

"Yah."

"Try to cut in front of 'em."

"Can't do it, mister."

Every time an opening occurred the ambulance would weave and sprint ahead. Its driver realized what I intended, and in turn I had a pretty fair idea of what he had in mind once he discovered that he couldn't run away from us. The crazy irony of it was that I couldn't think of any way to beat him. Two police cars passed us and paid no attention. Waving at them would have been completely useless. They assumed the cab carried a doctor or a member of the family. Even my Polish friend was getting worried. "Ram them when you see another cop," I said.

"They'll get away, mister."

Even a New York cab with heavy duty bumpers has a vulnerable nose, while almost any car except a Volkswagen can take a wallop in the rear and keep on going. Explanations, even to a wide awake policeman, would have taken much too long and very possibly might not have been believed at all. I wasn't sleepy anymore and didn't feel the heat, but I was grinning with frustration, long before the utterly inevitable happened. That was out in Suffolk County, beyond Massapequa, on a winding side road off State Highway 89 with only farmhouses in view and traffic thinned out to a passing car every other mile or so. They'd killed the siren, but they were still doing fifty in the curves, and then around the next one there they were, of course, slewed right across both lanes, and with an automatic rifle staring at us through the driver's open window. You don't argue with an M16. You stop, and get out nice and easy, and you show your empty hands. You smile as if you love the world. You do all that, knowing full well the driver's partner will come up behind you, to one side, out of the field of fire, and that he has a blackjack and will knock you cold.

The big surprise turned out to be Dr. Juan Ruiz-Martinez, late of Bogotá, Colombia.

I recognized him right away when I woke up. You're not supposed to be particularly with it after you've been sapped, but that depends a lot on who took care of you. The artist knows his tool, and knows where to apply it. He can kill you with it, painlessly and without effort, or he can administer a dose of anesthetic that'll hold you for a certain length of time, allowing for a reasonable margin. You may wind up with a headache or a lump, or both, according to your physical condition and his preference. I had a little buzzing in my ears, but I was fine, comparatively speaking. Judging by the twilight, they had let me have about five hours' sleep I badly needed, on a quilted-vinyl covered, medical examination table in a good-sized doctor's office, furnished pleasantly enough with walls of bookshelves and a modern lucite desk placed at three-quarters' profile to the picture window. From behind this desk the radical little physician I had cheated of his revolution, just about two years ago, regarded me across the hands he'd folded to support his chin. It was a level stare, lacking in satisfaction or displeasure. When he spoke, I noticed that his English had improved a lot. "You may as well sit up, sir. You have not been seriously hurt."

I swung my legs off the examination table. There were a few seconds of mild dizziness. The picture window framed a stretch of formal lawn, a brick wall topped with broken glass and an uninteresting sunset. In the doorway on my right, the ambulance attendants leaned against one of the book-lined walls, dispassionately watching me.

". . . Where's my cab driver?"

Dr. Ruiz-Martinez used a thumbnail on his tiny black mustache. But he succeeded very nicely in conveying an impression of professional dignity. It's difficult to entertain respect for anybody who believes in such a pompous bandit and vulgarian as Fidel Castro. Just the same, you had to hand it to this man. He'd managed to get into the U.S., no doubt illegally, and to set up an espionage safe house in a private booby hatch, abortion clinic, or old ladies' home, no doubt located somewhere on Long Island. Or it had been set up for him.

"Both of you will be released tomorrow," he informed me coolly.

"Why not now?"

"Because a little time is needed, my dear Mr. Harvester."

"For what?"

It was a silly question, since I wanted him to think I wasn't functioning too well just yet. The answer stood before me, in the middle of the parquet floor, between the desk and the examination table. Señora Maria de Cardozo's pigskin trunk apparently had not been opened. It looked flashy in this room, and decadent, like a kept showgirl in high boots and leather miniskirt and carrying a yellow riding crop.

He wanted me to realize that it was going to be stashed away. Securely. This could be arranged, even if those who knew about it should be caught. Not easily, and not for very long, but long enough to serve its purpose, I suspected. The two men in white were noticeably getting bored with me. I'd given them a problem earlier that afternoon, but now I talked and acted like a clown.

"You boys are Cubans, aren't you?"

They ignored that. On the wall between them leaned the automatic rifle, casually handy. I looked at the driver's partner, bared a tooth, and said mendaciously: "You owe me a bad headache, fellow."

They paid no attention to that either, but the man behind

the desk leaned back and frowned at me. "There is no point in personal recriminations," he said quietly. "What you have stumbled upon will, within the next few weeks, completely change the world."

"It will?"

He was convinced of it, sincerely and entirely, I could see. Some of us are good liars; some of us can make like Richard Burton. But not he, as I remembered very well indeed. Right now he was as honestly concerned about the situation and about the need for me to understand it as he would have been about his mother's funeral. "As you must know," he said, "all wars are won by persuasion. It is necessary for the winner to convince the loser of the fact that he has lost. That to continue to resist would be unthinkable."

"So?"

"Rabies, Mr. Harvester, induces violent insanity before it kills. Its virus normally has a long incubation period and can be suppressed by vaccination, even after it has been transmitted. But the special culture we have imported will incubate in man in half an hour. Its transmission is by air, like influenza. Vaccination is effective only if supplied preventively."

"It kills in half an hour?"

He shook his head, impatient with me. "No, sir. In five days."

"But half an hour after infection you're a raving lunatic?"

"That is correct."

I caught myself taking a fairly deep and sudden breath. "You're saying, doctor, that what you can do is create hell on earth. By opening that trunk."

His silence lasted a long time. He was still making up his mind about me. Finally he sighed, as if resigned to it that I would have to do. "You are a highly reputable journalist as well as an intelligence operative, Mr. Harvester. You may inform the people of the world that if the government of the

United States, the Soviet Russian government, and their respective allies will disarm within six weeks, this hell on earth of yours will be avoided.''

"Will it? What'll take its place?''

"The People's Democratic Government of China, Mr. Harvester,'' he told me, with unconscious humor. "And its allies.''

I got down off the examination table. The parquet floor felt like glass under my feet as I stood looking down at the Cardozo trunk. "That's what I thought. The Chinese, and you fellows. You're the only ones who just might manage vaccinating your whole population secretly. If there's a simple oral vaccine for this bug.'' He nodded, almost eagerly, and started to assure me that there was indeed, but I held up my hand. "Also,'' I said, "both they and you consider yourselves preordained as well as fully qualified to keep the rest of us in line. So do the Russians, for that matter. But they've always been a little more, uh, shall we say conservative?''

He wasn't really worried yet. He didn't need me to be nice to him. He could just turn me loose, as advertised, tomorrow, and sit back to wait for me to pass the word.

The only possibility he seemed to have neglected to take into account was that I might prove to be purposefully disagreeable.

I turned my back on him and took a step in the direction of the door where the two Cubans leaned against the wall and watched me woodenly. They were as nervous about me as if I'd turned into a pussy cat. I was as big as they were but a good many years older, and my knees were wobbling, they could see. I had no weapons on me, and I talked a lot of foolishness. "If I'm supposed to help, you wouldn't want to shoot me, would you, boys? Besides, we need to be a little careful with that thing around. Don't we?''

They glanced at where my thumb was pointing backward. They weren't going to shoot me, or at least not in this room. The notion wouldn't have occurred to them. The gun was there because they'd brought it in with them, that afternoon. I took another carefully uncertain step in their direction, and the driver said, almost goodnaturedly: *"No hay de qué, señor.* Maybe you sleep a leetle more, eh? You don' look so good."

"Oh, I'm okay," I said, and took another step, a long one, rammed the finger lance of my right arm into his stomach, kneed him in the face when he collapsed. His partner had the blackjack off his hip and up, by then, ready to deal with me. I laughed at him. He was a specialist, an artist. He could take me only if I would hold still for him. A surgeon with a scalpel would have been about as useful in a fight. I grabbed his wrist and wrenched his arm out of its socket, choked the scream of pain before it left his throat, and slammed his head into the bookcase wall. He toppled over on the body of the driver, but he still had enough left in him to scrabble for the M16. I snatched it off the floor and crashed the butt into his jaw, and came up very fast in a low crouch to level it at Dr. Juan Ruiz-Martinez. I had half expected to be forced to shoot it out with him, he'd had a pistol in his desk drawer in Bogotá, but he was leaning back, unruffled, empty-handed, dignified.

Between us, undisturbed, and looking quite as flashily depraved as it had looked before, stood the Señora Maria de Cardozo's pigskin trunk.

"There now," I said. "That *is* a little better. Now pick up that phone, please, doctor. Dial 0 for Operator. Ask her for the FBI."

He shrugged, reached for the instrument, and dialed. I got up out of my crouch and kept him covered, but he didn't look at me or at the rifle muzzle. He was staring pensively out of the window, at the sunset and the empty lawn. The phone stopped burring, and the operator's cricket voice came on. His own spoke quietly, very much under control. He did not ask her for the FBI. "I wish to place a transatlantic call, please." When I took a step toward the desk and gestured with the rifle

barrel he held up his hand, still without looking at me. He appeared to be so certain of himself I actually felt a chill of consternation. "This is Doctor Ruiz at the Sanatorium Montevista,
Massapequa, New York, Area Code 617, Number 223-6235.
I wish to speak with the yacht *Miss Virginia*, in port at
Cannes, in France. The number of the dockside telephone connection there is six-eight-two. Ask for Miss Yuri Franklin,
please." He pushed the phone across the desk and held out the
receiver to me.

It was obvious by then exactly what they had in mind. I
tucked the M16 under my arm, and walked around the pigskin
trunk. I took the phone with my left hand. She sounded gay,
and charmingly affectionate. "Surprised, Steve Harvester?"

"No. You were using me. I knew it. I enjoyed it."

That earned me the silver tinkle of her laughter. "Did you
really? Are you going to cooperate with us?"

"You're Chinese, aren't you?"

"Yes, darling, of course. The Franklin girl had buck teeth,
and she needed glasses. But she *was* an anthropologist."

"Sure, Captain Wahlstrom found that out," I said. "It's
what he came to tell me at the Rif Hotel."

The silver bell was silenced. "You just guessed that."

"No, Miss Franklin. It's my Navajo great-grandmother. She
tells me that you also had Leon de Bas shut down, after you'd
let him in on Dancing Dog. She even tells me why."

"Please hold the phone," Yuri said coolly, and in a few seconds Lita's voice came to my ear. She sounded just as if this
were a private call between us, with no hint of trouble. "Steve,
how soon will you be back?"

"That's hard to say. Maybe the day after tomorrow. It
depends."

"They want me to explain to you that they have taken over
here. Most of the crew had gone on shore leave, and the officer on watch is dead. They've locked up the two stewards and

the radioman on duty. I'm supposed to be a hostage.''

"Yes, I gathered that.''

"They say that you've met two of them. There's one who's named Jean-Claude. He has an older brother. You're not going to give in to them, are you?''

"I love you very much,'' I said. "You've never really known that, not before last night. But you do know it now. Whatever happens, you must know I love you. . . . Hello, Miss Franklin, can you hear me?''

The little silver bell was back in working order. "But of course I can, Steve Harvester. You *are* a sentimentalist. And now you'll do what Dr. Ruiz wants you to do, won't you?''

"No, Miss Franklin,'' I said slowly. "No, I won't. This Dancing Dog of yours may be the real thing, but I don't think so. You don't need the real thing to pull this off. You just need me. And you've been operating on me since before we met last Friday night, in Tangier, haven't you?''

". . . Have I, darling?''

"Sure you have. You set me up for this, kid. Shame on you, trying to put on an old man. Shame on your bosses in Peking. Stealing a week of my vacation. Killing other agents right in front of me, just so I'd take you seriously. Chasing me four thousand miles out of my way to get me into bed with Dr. Ruiz. If I play your game, people are going to *believe* in Dancing Dog. They'll be afraid of it. That's what you want, because the fear of hell is just as bad as hell itself. So you might win, and we don't need that.''

"Don't we, darling? But you'll have to play our game, won't you?''

I could see why she would assume so, while she had her hands on Lita. "Look,'' I said. "You did a good job. I was buying tickets to the show all week. But here you've got me up on stage, where I can see the props too close. This Chinese box of yours has to be empty. Germs are tricky to transport, and dangerous if there's a little accident. And you're not really looking for two billion corpses. You want all those bodies live and healthy, working for you, kowtowing to you. Forget it. It'll never happen. You yourself should know that much, but in Peking they've always had peculiar ideas about us foreign devils."

"You," said Yuri Franklin icily, "are talking too much, aren't you, Steve Harvester?"

I looked up at the man in the white jacket. "What's your professional opinion, doctor? The young lady thinks I'm nervous." He stared back at me uneasily. I laid down the receiver of the phone before him on the desk. "Go on, doctor. Tell her." He shook his head. I put the muzzle of the M16 against his upper lip and hooked the front sight into his left nostril, ripping it. The blood sprayed down into his lap. "Tell her!" He clapped a handkerchief over his nose and started reaching for the phone. The muzzle of the M16 jabbed at his hand. "Don't touch that. Just speak up."

"You are a Fascist hoodlum," he said loudly. "But you are not nervous."

"Thank you, doctor. Now inform the lady that I've got a gun, if you don't mind."

"He has a gun."

"And that the trunk is in the room with us." He hesitated, sensing what I had in mind. The M16 explored the kneehole of his desk. Its safety catch clicked off. He flinched away from it.

"The trunk is here."

I said: "So listen. In exactly sixty seconds I'll pick up that phone. If the Señora de Vargas answers it, and tells me that she is alone and well on *Miss Virginia*, and if I believe her, fine. I'll go away and take the bundle with me. There's a nice, big ocean and a fishing port with charter boats about ten miles from here. But if she doesn't answer or she doesn't sound just right, I'll fire a clip into this Dancing Dog of yours. You wouldn't like that. Both of you would lose a lot of face, back home."

From the receiver on the desk a cricket stridence of protest began to rasp. Dr. Ruiz ignored it. "My dear sir, you've lost your mind," he solemnly assured me. "You cannot wipe out three-quarters of the population of the world to save one woman of your choice."

"That's not my problem, doctor. It's Miss Franklin's. I'm a sentimentalist, remember? Can she take a chance on me?" I laughed at him, and at the instrument that carried off our conversation on four thousand miles of underwater cable, radio relay, or satellite bounceback, they never tell you which. It was a fairly nasty laugh. "Get with it, both of you. There's nothing in this for you but to cop out of the situation. If I drop that trunk in the Atlantic, that'll do it. You can say it never was delivered, that the airline really lost it. You can fix your underlings to back you up. But if we shoot the works, right here and now, you've had it. Whether Dancing Dog's a phony or the real article will make no difference. Not to you, after your masters get through with you. Let's start a countdown. Sixty seconds. Fifty-nine. Fifty-eight. Fifty-seven . . ."

On the desk, the cricket sputtered briefly, then fell silent. Dr. Ruiz seemed to have his bloody nose under control. It took both hands, as I'd intended that it should.

At thirty-five I stopped the countdown and reached for the phone.